Praise for Robin Lee Hatcher

"Romantic fare perfect for curling up in front of the fireplace with a cup of hot chocolate."
—*Library Journal* on *Hearts Evergreen*

"Hatcher knows what the reader wants and always delivers."
—*RT Book Reviews* on *Fit to Be Tied*

Praise for Kathryn Springer

"Springer shows us through this delightful story that though we are unable to change our past, we can certainly learn from it. It is never too late for forgiveness and closure."
—*RT Book Reviews* on *The Prodigal's Christmas Reunion*

"Kathryn Springer's refreshing writing style and sense of humor make this story sing!"
—Neta Jackson, author of The Yada Yada Prayer Group series, on *Front Porch Princess*

ROBIN LEE HATCHER

is a winner of the Christy Award for Excellence in Christian Fiction, two RITA® Awards, two *RT Book Reviews* Career Achievement Awards and the Romance Writers of American Lifetime Achievement Award. She is the author of more than 60 novels and lives in Idaho.

KATHRYN SPRINGER

is a lifelong Wisconsin resident. Growing up in a "newspaper" family, she spent long hours as a child plunking out stories on her mother's typewriter and hasn't stopped writing since. She loves to write inspirational romance because it allows her to combine her faith in God with her love of a happy ending.

Hearts Evergreen

Robin Lee Hatcher
Kathryn Springer

Love Inspired

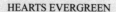  ™ LOVE INSPIRED BOOKS

Recycling programs for this product may not exist in your area.

ISBN-13: 978-0-373-78744-9

HEARTS EVERGREEN

Copyright © 2007 by Harlequin Books S.A.

The publisher acknowledges the copyright holders of the individual works as follows:

A CLOUD MOUNTAIN CHRISTMAS
Copyright © 2007 by Robin Lee Hatcher

A MATCH MADE FOR CHRISTMAS
Copyright © 2007 by Kathryn Springer

www.LoveInspiredBooks.com

Printed in U.S.A.

CONTENTS

A CLOUD MOUNTAIN CHRISTMAS

Robin Lee Hatcher

Chapter One

Maddie Scott's heart stopped in midbeat: SUPER BOWL MVP CRAIG HOUSTON WEDS ACTRESS SHARI WARD. COUPLE'S FIRST CHILD EX-PECTED IN FEBRUARY.

"Miss? Are you ready?"

She looked toward the convenience store clerk, trying to ignore the humming in her ears.

The girl frowned. "Are you ready to pay for those things?"

"Yes." Maddie grabbed the magazine and dropped it, a bag of chips and a soda onto the counter. "I'm ready."

The clerk looked at the magazine cover. "That guy's a hottie, huh?"

Please be quiet. Biting her tongue, Maddie pulled a twenty-dollar bill from her wallet and held it toward the girl, hoping that would hurry her along.

It worked. Two minutes later, Maddie pushed through the glass swinging door of the convenience store and hurried toward her rental car. She unlocked the driver-side door of the black SUV with the remote, longing to get inside, away from anyone's view.

As soon as the car door was open, she tossed her purchases onto the passenger seat, then slid behind the wheel.

It shouldn't matter. It *didn't* matter. Craig Houston hadn't been a part of her life for more than four years. Their five-year marriage had crumbled beneath the weight of his bad habits and extramarital affairs. Her love for him was killed slowly but surely long before the signatures were dry on the divorce papers that had ended both her marriage and her dreams for the future.

"I don't want kids, Maddie. I'm not cut out to be a dad."

Tears pooled in her eyes as the memory echoed in her mind.

The truth was, Craig hadn't wanted kids *with her*. He looked happy enough on the cover of that magazine with his pregnant bride.

She wiped away the tears with the back of her hand. Silly to get upset over this. It wasn't as if she didn't *know* Craig and that actress were an item. She'd have to be a nun in a French Alps monastery to be unaware. Their faces had been plastered in various magazines, week after week, the handsome NFL jock and the gorgeous Hollywood star.

It was the injustice of it all that stuck in Maddie's craw. Here she was, four years after the divorce, swimming in a sea of debt—the debt Craig had left her—and her ex-husband was living the high life.

She drew a deep breath. *God, don't let me give in to*

self-pity. I know that what Craig does and who he mar-ries has nothing to do with me. Help me to quit looking back. Help me to trust You with my future. She turned the key in the ignition and backed the SUV out of its parking place.

By force of will, Maddie turned her thoughts to the reason for her trip into the snowy Idaho mountains. There were still two hours to go until her destination. If she did her job, the resulting commission could wipe out her debt. Wouldn't that make this her best Christmas in years?

And there was one added benefit. Tucked away in the mountains of Idaho, she needn't worry about run-ning into Craig and his new bride on the streets of L.A.

Tony Anderson took several steps backward and stared at the Christmas tree in the corner of the lobby. Colored lights twinkled, reflecting off tinsel, gar-land and ornaments. Empty boxes, wrapped like gifts, peeked from beneath the lower limbs of the fragrant pine tree.

"What do you think, Audrey?"

"It's a work of art. Prettiest I've seen in this place in ages."

"Good enough to make the guests feel festive for the holidays, anyway." He glanced at his watch. "Speaking of guests, is the room ready for Mr. Fairchild?"

"It's ready. Got the new sheets and comforter on the bed and fresh towels in the bathroom. Don't you worry. He'll get the royal treatment while he's here."

"I can always count on you."

Audrey Tremaine was a godsend, no doubt about it. She had worked at the lodge for forty-two years, starting as a maid when she was twenty years old. Although she now wore the title of head housekeeper, she did more than keep the place clean and tidy. She pretty much ran it, from manning the front desk to hiring part-time help to making their guests feel at home.

Of course, until they had more guests, it wasn't all that hard for Audrey to manage the lodge. But if the manuscript brought the price some thought it would, Tony wouldn't have to worry about money. He was eager to see if David Fairchild agreed with others. If he did, if Fairchild purchased the manuscript for the kind of money Tony hoped for, the renovations of Cloud Mountain Lodge wouldn't take years to complete. He wouldn't have to do the majority of the work himself. The lodge could be bigger and better than his original plans. He had plenty of ideas. What he lacked to make them come true was cold hard cash.

"How about the rooms for the Sullivan family reunion?" He picked up the empty boxes that had held the Christmas decorations.

"We're on schedule. All you need is to get that paper hung in the green room."

"I was planning to do that later today." He headed down the hall toward the back door.

Audrey called after him, "Hurry back. Cookie made cornbread and a pot of chili for lunch. It's ready when you are."

"Sounds good. Be right back."

Cold air bit him the instant he stepped outside. He

hunched his shoulders as he strode down the steps and along the shoveled walkway to the shed. After tossing the empty boxes inside, he glanced toward the new metal building that housed a workshop, his Jeep and the used-but-new-to-him Sno-Cat.

All things considered, a great deal had been accomplished since last May when he took possession of the lodge. It felt good, watching it come together. Every day he thanked God for allowing him to live his dream.

He turned and strode back to the lodge, grateful for the warmth that greeted him.

"How was the drive, Miss Scott?" he heard Audrey say. "Were the roads clear?"

A woman replied, "Yes, they were dry almost the whole way. Thank goodness. I haven't driven in snow for years."

Tony walked toward the lobby, pausing when he reached the doorway.

Audrey stood behind the counter while the woman signed the check-in form. Three designer bags—well-worn but high quality—and a black leather briefcase sat on the hardwood floor near their guest's feet. She wore straightlegged jeans, snow boots and a white, down-filled parka.

Audrey handed a key card to the guest, spotting Tony as she did so. "Here he is now. Miss Scott, this is Mr. Anderson, the man who found the manuscript. Tony, this is Mr. Fairchild's representative. She came in his place."

Before the woman turned completely around, before Tony saw more than a glimpse of her profile, he recognized her. Maddie Scott. Her straight black hair was longer. She looked a little thinner. But it was Maddie.

She wouldn't recognize him, of course. Why should she? He'd been just another guy in college, occasionally hanging around the edges of her life. No competition for the football star who'd captured her heart.

"Hello, Mr. Anderson." She took a step toward him, her hand extended, a warm smile in her voice. "I'm Maddie Scott. Mr. Fairchild sends his apologies for not being able to be here. His plans changed abruptly, and rather than postpone the meeting, he sent me to represent his interests."

Tony took hold of her hand, wondering if it was good news or bad that David Fairchild hadn't come in person. "Welcome to Cloud Mountain, Ms. Scott. It's nice to have you here." That part he didn't have to wonder about. It was nice to see Maddie again, even if she didn't remember him.

"Thank you." She glanced around the lobby. "Looks like you're ready for Christmas."

"Pretty much. Next year we'll do more." Especially if this deal comes together the way I hope it will.

A frown furrowed her brow as she looked up at him. "I'm sorry, Mr. Anderson, but do I know you?"

That gave his ego a lift. Maybe he wasn't completely forgettable. "Call me Tony. Everybody does."

She continued to stare.

"We met in college."

"At Boise State?"

He nodded.

"Tony Anderson," she said softly, shaking her head.

Then her eyes lit with recognition as she pointed at him. "Anthony Anderson. History of Western Civilization. You used to hang around with Brad Taylor."

Tony nodded again.

"You look different. Didn't you wear glasses?"

"That was me."

"Contacts?"

"Laser surgery." He stepped to her bags, stuck one beneath his left arm, the briefcase beneath his right and grabbed the other two suitcases by their handles. "I'll show you to your room."

They climbed the curved staircase.

"So, are you from here, Tony?"

"No. I grew up on a farm near Twin Falls. But my aunt and uncle had a cabin up here for many years. My folks and I came up a lot when I was a kid. Went fishing and rode horses in the summer, went skiing and snow-mobiling in the winter." He glanced over his shoulder. "The lodge was already in decline back then, but I was a kid. To me, it was cool."

They arrived at the blue room.

"This is your room. I hope you'll find it to your liking."

"I'm sure I will." She slid the key card into the slot and removed it. The green light flashed and she pushed open the door. "Oh, this is lovely." She walked across the room to gaze out the window.

"Call the desk if you need anything." Tony set her bags inside the door. "Did Audrey tell you we were about to sit down to lunch? We'd like for you to join us if you're ready to eat."

"Thanks." She turned toward him. "I'd like that. I am hungry."

That's when he noticed the difference in her, something he hadn't seen earlier. There was sadness in her wide brown eyes, a deep kind of sadness that made his heart ache. And he knew who'd put it there: Craig Houston.

Chapter Two

Maddie sat on the bed and flipped open her mobile phone. Good. She had service. She hadn't been sure she would in these mountains. She pressed the number for David on her speed dial and waited for him to pick up.

"Maddie. Are you at the lodge already?"

"Yes. I got in a short while ago. I'm in my room and am about to go down for lunch."

"Have you met Mr. Anderson? What's your take on him?"

She rose and walked to the window again. The view was breathtaking. "Yes, we met. In fact, it turns out I know him. Sort of."

"What?"

"We went to college together, but I don't remember much about him. We didn't move in the same circles."

The Tony Anderson she remembered was more of a math geek, a rather shy kid with shaggy hair, a slender build and glasses, the sort who spent most Friday nights at the library instead of on dates. But that didn't describe the guy who'd escorted her up from the lobby a short while before. This Tony Anderson was confident and rugged with a great smile and the most striking blue eyes she'd ever seen.

David cleared his throat. "Is this going to help us or hurt us?"

She shook her head, more to shake off the image in her mind than in answer to David's question. "I don't think it will make a difference one way or the other. Don't worry. I'll close this deal before the weekend is over."

"I'm sure you will. You always do."

She hoped he was right. She owed David Fairchild, big time. He and his wife had been her good friends long before David became her employer. In some ways, he was the father she never knew.

Maddie turned to face her room again, staring at the four-poster bed, complete with blue and white canopy. "David, I saw the magazine cover with Craig and Shari on it."

There was a lengthy pause on the other end of the line. "I'm sorry you heard about it that way. I didn't know myself until this morning or I'd have warned you."

"It's okay." She released a sigh. "I was a little surprised about the baby on the way. How'd they manage to keep that out of the news for so long?"

"I don't know. But I do know this. The guy's an idiot. I've met Miss Ward. She's all flash and no substance. Craig's going to be miserable in no time."

"Thanks, David." She smiled sadly. "I'm sure it's

wrong of me to like that you said so, but I like it anyway."

He chuckled.

"I'd better go. I've got work to do."

"Well, don't forget to have a good time while you're there. You're in danger of becoming a workaholic. You're young. Live a little."

They said goodbye and Maddie closed the cover of her phone. Her gaze shifted to her briefcase, but the growling of her stomach intruded on thoughts of work. Lunch first. Work later.

She hoped the food was good.

"She's a pretty thing." Audrey took plates and bowls from the sideboard and carried them to one of the smaller round tables. "How well did you know her?"

That was one of the negatives about living in a small town—everybody thought your business was theirs. But Tony didn't try to avoid the question. No point. She would worm it out of him eventually. "Not as well as I wanted to."

"Carrying a torch, huh?"

"No." The word felt like a lie, but it wasn't. Oh, he'd thought about Maddie through the years. How could he help it with her photos, along with Craig's, in magazines and newspapers, especially during football season.

Then came her divorce.

He felt sorry for her. It had to be rough, having your troubles become fodder for a gossip-hungry world. Tony had made more than his share of mistakes, but thankfully, only a handful of people knew about them. When he asked forgiveness or made amends for something, at least the press didn't take pictures and talk-show hosts didn't make jokes.

"Come in, Miss Scott," Audrey said, intruding on Tony's thoughts. "You're right on time."

He turned to watch Maddie enter the dining room. *Ker-thump.*

The sensation in his chest was oddly familiar. Familiar because it had happened often around Maddie during his college years. Odd because he hadn't felt it in eight or nine years.

Audrey motioned toward the table. "We serve our meals family style, although Tony's planning for the day when we can operate a full-fledged restaurant again."

He pulled out a chair for Maddie. "Here you go." He felt like a tongue-tied teenager and that wasn't good. He had business to do with this woman. Important business.

Ker-thump.

Just as Maddie sat at the table, the door to the kitchen swung open and Cookie entered the dining room, carrying a serving bowl filled with chili and a platter of corn bread.

Cookie's real name was Jacob Smitherman, although few people knew it. In his youth, he was a logger, but an accident left him with a bad leg. That's when he turned to cooking, first for loggers in the camps, later—having perfected his craft—in restaurants across the Northwest. A desire to retire in the central Idaho mountains had brought him to the lodge, for which Tony was more than a little grateful.

Audrey introduced Maddie as Cookie set the bowl of chili on the table.

"Glad to have you with us," the older man said to Maddie. "I hear you're from Los Angeles."

"I am now, but I grew up in Idaho."

Cookie took a seat at the table. And, with everyone settled, Tony looked toward Maddie. "I like to say grace before we eat when it's just the staff. Do you mind?"

She shook her head.

Tony closed his eyes. "Lord, we thank You for this food and for the hands that prepared it. Bless it to the nourishment of our bodies so that we might do the work You've called us to do. Amen." When he looked up, he found Maddie watching him again, this time with the slightest of smiles bowing her mouth.

Ker-thump.

Maddie couldn't remember the last time she sat down to eat with a group of strangers who said grace over their food. Of course, she usually dined alone or on the go and her own prayers were often forgotten in her haste.

"So tell us, Miss Scott." The chef held the serving bowl toward her. "Why on earth did you leave Idaho to live in California?"

She scooped chili into a large ceramic bowl. "My husband's job took us there."

"You're married?" Audrey looked as surprised as she sounded. "And here I was, calling you Miss Scott. I'm sorry."

Maddie shook her head. "I should have said *ex*-husband. I'm divorced. And Scott was my maiden name."

"Oh, dear. How very sad about your marriage. Divorce is a hard thing to go through."

She realized then that Audrey Tremaine didn't know who her ex-husband was. Didn't know who *she* was. It was nice not to be recognized, nice not to have people whispering behind her back. *Isn't that Maddie Scott? Tsk, tsk. Couldn't keep her husband from cheating. What's wrong with her, do you suppose?*

She drew a quick breath, trying to ignore the welling hurt and frustration. She hated feeling this way. It wasn't even about Craig anymore. It was the sense of failure and inadequacy that ate at her.

As if sensing Maddie's turmoil, Audrey changed the subject. "Tony, why don't you tell Ms. Scott how you found the manuscript?"

"She probably knows the story from Mr. Fairchild."

"No, not really. Please tell me." Maddie would listen to him read the telephone book if it would prevent another bout of self-pity.

Tony smiled as he spread honey-butter on a square of cornbread. "Well, if you're sure it won't bore you."

"I'm sure."

"I'd worked fixing up the lodge about a month when I got to the room at the end of the hall on the second floor of the east wing. The former owners said nobody'd stayed in it since Small's death back in the late fifties. He made this lodge his home for more than twenty years."

Maddie knew a little about the reclusive writer. His

most famous works were published in the late 1920s, but there'd been demand for his new efforts—which were few and far between—in the latter years of his life.

"The rumors that he died from foul play kept guests out of that room. Some said he haunts the room where he was murdered."

"I don't believe in ghosts." Maddie squared her shoulders. Did Tony think he would get more for the manuscript if there was something spooky about where it was found? If so, she was surprised. It didn't fit with a man who said thanks to God for his food. Still, she was nobody's fool. She would be careful.

Tony grinned, as if reading her thoughts. "Neither do I. Besides, the research I've done proves Small died of natural causes."

She relaxed a little.

"Anyway, like I said, Small lived in that room until his death. Three of the walls had built-in bookshelves and there was a built-in desk beneath one of the two windows in the room. It was when I started tearing things out that I found the manuscript. The pages were tied with string, like a present. About five hundred pages or so—" he used his hands to indicate the thickness of the manuscript "—all yellowed and scribbled on with notes, changes, doodles. He'd scrawled his name across the first page, too."

"Tony almost threw out the whole bunch," the housekeeper interjected. "He thought it was junk."

He nodded. "Came pretty close to it. I'm thankful Audrey suggested I have somebody look at it before I did."

"And now he has a number of people interested in buying it." Audrey reached over and patted the back of Tony's hand.

Was this lady for real? Or were the two of them working her, hoping to up the price?

Maddie dropped her gaze to her bowl, wondering when she'd become a cynic. Whenever it was, she didn't like it much.

Chapter Three

Tony watched as Maddie dabbed the corners of her mouth with the cloth napkin, then placed it on the table beside her empty bowl.

"That was delicious, Cookie." She slid the chair back from the table and stood.

The chef accepted the compliment with a brief nod.

Maddie looked at Tony. "If you'll excuse me, I need to get unpacked. What time should we meet to go over Mr. Fairchild's offer?"

So that's how it was? Down to business, just like that. Although he knew he shouldn't expect otherwise—it was why Maddie came to Cloud Mountain Lodge. Still, Tony wanted to delay the start of the negotiations. Maybe because he feared talking business would bring about her departure too soon. Or maybe because he wanted to make her smile again, a smile that reached into her big brown eyes, a smile that he remembered from college.

He placed his napkin on the table. "You're going to be here for four days. There's plenty of time for us to meet. How about we do it in the morning? This afternoon I need to run into town for supplies and then I've got to hang wallpaper. We've got more guests coming in over the weekend."

"Well…"

"You had a long drive up from Boise. Kick back and relax a bit. That's what a place like Cloud Mountain is all about. Relaxing. Enjoying the beauty around us."

"I suppose you're right. Morning it is, then."

Audrey began to gather the dirty dishes to carry into the kitchen. "There's a lovely fire in the fireplace in the reading room. It's right off the lobby. Once you've got things settled, come on down and enjoy the view. I'll fix you a cup of coffee, if you'd like."

"She prefers hot tea with milk," Tony said.

Maddie turned her head sharply. "How did you know that?"

"I heard you say so."

"When?"

He shrugged, making light of the memory. "I was part of a study group that met in the student union building. You know how those groups were crowded on top of each other. I must have overheard you tell the waitress." He rose from his chair. "I'd better pick up those supplies or I'll never finish that room on time."

He strode from the dining room, mentally calling himself several kinds of a fool. "Anderson, you've got more important things to think about than her."

Only, what were they?

Maddie took her time unpacking, hanging clothes in the closet, placing other things in the bureau drawers.

Her personal care items—favorite brand of shampoo, face cleanser, lotions, makeup—went in the bathroom. As she turned her attention to the materials in her brief-case, she remembered David's admonition: *Well, don't forget to have a good time while you're there. You're in danger of becoming a workaholic. You're young. Live a little.*

A sigh escaped her lips. David was right. All she did was work. She had no social life to speak of. Even her involvement at church was minimal. When some-one asked her to go to brunch after Sunday service or to come to a women's Bible study or small group meet-ing, her reply was always the same: "I'm sorry. I have work to do. Maybe next time?"

But next time never came, she was busy then, too.

Maddie sank onto the bed. "Why am I like this?"

Because you're afraid to live.

It was true. She was afraid. Afraid of failing…again. Afraid of never being free of the past. Afraid that she wouldn't climb out of debt. Afraid to trust others. Afraid to trust herself.

Afraid to trust God.

It hurt to confess her lack of trust, even silently. She knew it shouldn't be that way. She knew God loved her and cared about her present and her future. But still she was afraid to let down her guard, to embrace her life as it was, as it was yet to be.

As she'd done several times since her arrival, she walked to the large window and looked at the beautiful winter scenery beyond the glass. So different from Los Angeles. She should listen to David. She should take the time to enjoy herself while she was here. Maybe get into the Christmas spirit.

Christmas.

As a child, she'd loved this season—the lights, the hidden presents, the trees, the parties—but now she dreaded it. The month of December was filled with bad memories. Broken promises. Ugly arguments. Shattered expectations. And like icing on a cruel cake, her divorce had also become final in December.

She hadn't been in the Christmas spirit since. Her world had been reduced to work, work and more work.

I don't want to be like this any longer, God. Help me, please.

Tony was loading the last of the supplies into the back of the Jeep when he saw Maddie coming down the sidewalk on the opposite side of the street, gazing at the window displays of the small shops that lined Cloud Mountain's main thoroughfare. She stopped outside Candy Corner.

Her white knit cap was pulled low over her ears and her hands were shoved into the pockets of her down coat. Even from across the street he could tell she was shivering, her shoulders hunched forward. Years in California must have thinned her blood.

He closed the back of the Jeep and headed across the street. When he stepped onto the curb, he asked, "Got a sweet tooth?"

She gasped as she whirled around. "Tony. You scared me half to death."

"Sorry." He grinned. "Didn't mean to."

"You don't look sorry." After a moment, she smiled, too.

"The caramel apples topped with nuts are my favorite. What about you?"

"Almond toffee."

"Come on." He jerked his head. "My treat."

"Oh, I shouldn't." She touched her hips. "Too many calories."

"A little won't hurt you. Besides you're so thin right now, a good gust of wind might blow you away."

"I don't know...."

He chuckled as he took her arm and steered her into the shop. The air inside was thick with wonderful, sweet smells.

"I've gained a pound already," she said.

Evie Barrett, the owner of Candy Corner, came out of the kitchen, wiping her hands on her apron as she approached them from the opposite side of the candy displays. "Hey, Tony. How you doin'?"

"Good, Evie." He motioned toward Maddie. "This is Maddie Scott. She's a guest at the lodge for the weekend."

"Nice to meet you, Maddie. This your first time to Cloud Mountain?"

"Yes."

"Have you been skiing yet?"

"No. I only arrived at the lodge a short while ago."

"I was up there with my sons yesterday after they got out of school. Great powder this week. You'll see what I mean when you get out there." She patted her fingertips on the display case. "What can I do for you?"

Tony answered, "We'll take a pound of the almond toffee and a half dozen of the caramel apples with nuts."

"Comin' right up."

Maddie looked at Tony as if he'd lost his mind. "A pound?"

He shrugged.

"I'm in so much trouble," she said beneath her breath.

He laughed.

She smiled in return.

If he could have captured that moment and kept it in a jar, he would have. It was perfect. The two of them, like old friends, smiling and laughing in a candy shop. It was his best dream come true.

Except in his best dream, they would be more than friends.

Slow down, Anderson.

He turned to watch Evie weigh the almond toffee on the scales.

He hadn't really *known* Maddie in college. He'd *wanted* to know her. So had plenty of other guys. But she never had eyes for anyone but Craig Houston. All Tony could do back then was stand on the sidelines and wish he were more like the football star.

But he was nothing like Craig, and he was glad of it. Maybe things could be different now. After all, God wasn't surprised when Maddie showed up at the lodge. Maybe this was part of His plan.

Or it could be wishful thinking.

Either way, it wouldn't hurt to find out which it was.

Tony paid for the candy, then motioned toward one of the small white tables that stood along the opposite wall. "Let's indulge."

"Okay. I shouldn't, but okay."

After they were seated, Tony handed her the bag of toffee. She reached inside and withdrew a piece. As she bit into it, her eyes twinkled in appreciation.

"That good, huh?"

She nodded. "That good." She popped the rest of the piece into her mouth.

"I suppose I shouldn't ask questions while you're eating."

"No. Go ahead. Save me from myself."

He leaned back in the chair. "I was wondering if you've still got family in Idaho."

"No." She shook her head. "My dad died when I was a toddler and Mom never remarried. When my sister, Kate, moved to Florida with her husband, Mom moved there, too. I was still with Craig at the time—" a shadow passed over her face "—and we were never home much. So it made sense for Mom to live near Kate." She took another piece of toffee from the bag. "What about you? What have you been doing since college?"

"I got my degree in business management and put it to use with a conglomerate down in Texas. I did well, but I missed Idaho. So when I heard the owner of the lodge wanted to sell, I started planning and saving. A few years later, I made him an offer."

"Is your family still in Twin Falls?"

"No. Mom and Dad both passed away while I was in Texas."

"I'm sorry. Was it an accident? They must have been rather young."

Tony twirled the stick on a caramel apple between his thumb and index finger. "Cancer took Mom six years ago. Dad had a heart attack a few months later."

"I'm sorry," she said again.

"Even after six years, there are still times when something happens and I think, wait until Mom and Dad hear about this." He shook his head slowly. "I guess you never completely get over losing your parents."

Silence stretched between them, each lost in thought.

Finally, Maddie said, "I'm assuming there's no Mrs. Tony Anderson."

"Not yet. But hopefully some day."

"Do you have some special girl in mind?"

How about you, Maddie?

It was crazy, how close he came to saying those words aloud. It was insane that he thought them at all. Maybe he'd better end this conversation before he made a complete fool of himself. He needed to get away from Maddie and breathe in some crisp winter air to clear his head so he could think straight again.

But when he opened his mouth, he said something unexpected. "Listen, why don't I skip hanging wallpaper and you skip the rest of your window shopping in beautiful downtown Cloud Mountain? Let's go skiing instead." He leaned toward her. "Let me show you why I wanted to move here and buy that old lodge."

She shook her head. "Tony, I haven't skied in years. I'm not sure I remember how. Besides, I don't have any gear."

"We can take care of all that. Skiing is like riding a bike. You don't forget. We'll take a nice easy run. No steep trails. No moguls."

"I don't know—"

"Come on. The sun is shining. The sky is clear. The snow is good. You'll have fun."

"Fun," she echoed softly, lowering her gaze to the bag of candy on the table. "Have some fun." When she looked up again, resolve filled her gaze. "Okay. Let's do it."

Chapter Four

Tony Anderson was a liar. Skiing was nothing like riding a bike.

Terror tightened Maddie's throat as the lift carried them higher up the mountainside.

Why did she agree to do this? Workaholism was at least safer! She was never comfortable on skis, never much good at it. She was much better at cheering others on from the warmth and safety of the lodge. Only the truly adventurous wanted to rocket down the side of a mountain on two toothpicks.

"Relax, Maddie."

She glanced at Tony. "Is it that obvious?"

"Afraid so."

"What happens when we get to the top? I don't remember how to get off this thing."

He pointed to where the lift deposited skiers before turning sharply for its return to the bottom of the mountain. "Just let your skis carry you off the seat and down the ramp. I'll be right beside you. You did fine down below. This isn't much different."

He was wrong about that. There was a great deal of difference between staying upright on the bunny slope and staying upright while plunging down the mountain she could see below.

Why did I listen to David? This isn't fun!

"Ready, Maddie? Here we go."

Was he kidding?

Somehow she found her skis flat against the ground and her bottom rising off the chairlift. Next thing she knew, she was down the ramp and stopped out of the way of the skiers who'd disembarked behind her.

"Good job." Tony grinned as he lowered his ski goggles into place. "Told you it wouldn't be hard."

She tried to return his smile, but it was a halfhearted effort.

God, get me down this mountain in one piece. Please.

Tony pointed with one of his poles. "That's the easiest trail on the front side of the mountain. I'll lead the way and set a nice, slow pace until you're comfortable."

I won't be comfortable until I'm back in the lodge.

"Ready?"

She nodded. "As ready as I'll ever be."

He pushed off in front of her, his skis gliding over the snow without a sound. Drawing a quick breath, she followed suit, albeit without the same fluidity of motion. It was obvious, even to Maddie's untrained eyes, that few skiers used this particular trail. Probably too tame, even for the kiddie set. Which meant it might be okay for her.

Hmm. This wasn't too bad. She was managing to

keep her skis parallel. Her knees were nicely flexed. No problem with the poles.

Lean. Turn. Glide.

Lean. Turn. Glide.

No, this wasn't bad at all.

Tall, snow-covered pine trees rose on either side of the track. Sunlight filtered through their branches, casting lacy shadows across the snow. Despite the frigid air, Maddie felt warm inside her snowpants, down-filled parka, knit cap and insulated gloves.

She might actually get to like this.

In front of her, Tony skied back and forth across the snow. About every third turn, he glanced back in her direction, no doubt to see if she'd fallen yet. This time when he looked back, she gave him a thumbs-up, letting him know she was A-okay.

Or not.

The almost level trail changed without warning. She felt the downward pull of the mountain. Her skis responded, moving faster over the snow. Maddie's heart quickened right along with the skis.

Too fast…too fast…too fast.

If Tony looked at her again, Maddie was too busy to notice. She needed her skis to behave.

Snowplow…snowplow…snow—

"Maddie!"

Her name on Tony's lips was the last thing that made sense to her. Then the world turned upside down and inside out. Her right ski went this way and her left ski went that way. She hit the ground—the snow wasn't nearly as soft as it looked—and felt it scrape her cheek before she tumbled, head over heels, for what seemed an eternity. She came to an abrupt halt at the base of an innocent-looking fir.

"Maddie?" Tony knelt beside her.

She looked up at him, dazed.

"Don't move yet. Let's make sure you're all in one piece."

Don't move. Was he kidding? With everything spinning like a top? She didn't want to ever move again.

"How many fingers am I holding up?"

She groaned. This wouldn't have happened if David Fairchild hadn't told her to have fun. Better hunched over her laptop than lying on her back in the snow while—

"Maddie? How many fingers?"

"Three. You're holding up three." This was too embarrassing for words. "I'm all right, Tony. The only thing hurt is my ego." She placed her elbows on the ground and pushed herself into a sitting position at the exact same moment her brain registered the pain shooting upward from her right leg. It stole her breath away. She dropped back to the ground.

"You're not all right."

Eyes closed, she clenched her teeth. "No."

"Where does it hurt?"

"My right leg. My ankle, I think. I don't know. I'm not sure. It hurts everywhere."

"We'll need a stretcher to get you down the mountain." He was silent a few moments. "I'll have to leave you alone while I get the Ski Patrol. There's nobody else in sight. Will you be okay?"

"Yes." She wondered if she sounded as uncertain as she felt.

"Let's get my coat around you. We don't want you taking a chill while I'm gone."

Maddie feared she might start to cry and the last thing she wanted to do was blubber like a baby in front of someone she had to negotiate with in the next few days.

"Here you go. I'll lift you up enough to slide the coat under your back. Ready? Here goes."

Tony's voice was quiet, but somehow it was strong, too. Her fears lessened.

"Can you open your eyes?" he asked. "I need you to look at me."

She complied.

"Now keep your eyes open. You need to stay alert. If someone comes down that trail, ask them to wait with you until I get back. I won't be long. I promise." He squeezed her hand, emphasizing his words.

"I'll be okay. Stop worrying and go."

He gave her a nod, his eyes filled with concern, and then he was gone, *swooshing* his way out of sight. The silence of the snowy mountain fell around her. She shivered, wishing she hadn't sent him away so soon.

It already seemed a long while since he'd left.

If this had been a downhill race, Tony might have given Bode Miller a run for his money. But no matter how fast he went, it wasn't fast enough. He remembered too well Maddie's pale face as she told him she would be okay. She hadn't looked okay. Pain had been evident in her big brown eyes.

Why hadn't he listened to her when she'd said she wasn't a good skier? Why hadn't he been content to buy her a treat in the candy shop?

Simple. Because he'd wanted to spend time with her. He'd wanted to enjoy her company before they got down to the business of haggling over the Uriah Small manuscript. She'd only be here four days and he'd wanted to make the most of them. Skiing seemed the natural option. It was, after all, why people came to Cloud Mountain, to ski and enjoy the great outdoors.

Still, her accident was his fault.

"Idiot."

As soon as he reached the base of the mountain, Tony contacted the volunteer Ski Patrol. Next he asked the lift operator to call Dr. Martin and make sure he was waiting for them at the clinic. Then Tony got back on the chairlift, anxious to reach Maddie, hating the thought of her lying there alone in the snow, cold and scared.

Relief overwhelmed him when he turned a bend in the trail and saw two other skiers waiting with Maddie. As he drew closer, he recognized them. Gary and Betina Patterson. The brother and sister, both in their early twenties, had moved to Cloud Mountain this past summer to manage the local hardware store for their great-grandfather, Jake Patterson.

Gary saw Tony and came to meet him. "She told us you'd be here any minute."

"How's she doing?"

"In pain but trying not to show it."

"The patrol should be right behind me." He skied forward. "I'm back, Maddie. We'll have you down the hill soon." He knelt across from Betina. "I know you're hurting. I'm sure sorry it happened. I shouldn't have brought you up on the lift. You were doing fine down below."

She gave him a game smile. "It isn't your fault. I could have declined your invitation."

"Right now, I wish you had."

She winced. "Right now, me, too."

In honor of the Christmas season, Maddie opted for a red moon boot on her broken ankle. If she had to be miserable, she might as well be festively fashionable.

"No weight on that leg for two weeks," Dr. Martin told her as he dried his hands. "Use the crutches. Fortunately, the break is in the distal fibula and doesn't involve the ankle joint itself. You should be able to get around without crutches in a couple of weeks."

"I'm supposed to drive back to Boise on Monday."

"Sorry, young lady. No driving for now."

"But—"

"No driving." The doctor shook his head. "Not for at least two weeks."

Wasn't that just terrific? How was she supposed to get back to L.A. if she couldn't drive? It wasn't like Cloud Mountain had an airport where she could catch a flight. What would she do with herself for two weeks? Her negotiations with Tony wouldn't take but a couple of days. And then what? Besides, she couldn't afford to be away from the office for that long. There was no way she could stay here for two weeks. She would have to hire a car service.

"How long will I be in this boot?"

"Six to eight weeks."

Perfect. Just perfect.

"Don't worry about where you'll stay," Tony offered. "We'll move you to one of the rooms on the ground floor. It isn't as nice as the one you're in now, but you'll be comfortable there. Audrey and I will make sure you don't need for anything."

Maddie cringed on the inside. How could she be a tough negotiator if Tony thought her needy and helpless? There must be something else she could say, something else she could do. She pressed a hand against her forehead, trying to focus her thoughts. If she could think straight—

"Take another one of these pain pills when you get back to the lodge." The doctor spoke to Maddie, but he handed the prescription bottle to Tony. "They'll make you sleepy, but that's a good thing. It'll keep you down and your leg elevated."

But I'm not supposed to be sleeping. I'm supposed to be working.

"I'll send in a wheelchair to see you out to your car."

Maddie hadn't the energy to do anything but nod.

Chapter Five

The pain in her ankle, combined with the narcotics Dr. Martin prescribed, caused time to pass in a blur. Whenever Maddie awoke from her drug-induced sleep, Audrey Tremaine was somewhere nearby, waiting to attend to her needs.

In one of her more lucid moments, Maddie called David to tell him what had happened to her. "But don't worry," she added at the end of her tale. "I'll wrap up this deal in a few days."

"I'm not worried about that. I'm worried about you. Are you sure you're getting proper care?" His voice sounded fuzzy and distant. "Is there anything you need?"

"Mmm."

"Maddie?"

Darkness threatened at the edge of consciousness, then spun inward, narrowing the light until it was a mere pinprick. "I need to go now." Without saying goodbye, she closed the cell phone and left it on the pillow as she drifted into a place of strange dreams.

* * *

Tony stared at the screen on his office computer. He was supposed to be attending to bookkeeping chores, but his thoughts were down the hall in the unfinished guestroom where Maddie lay sleeping. That's pretty much all she'd done in the two days since the accident.

With a groan, he leaned back in his chair and stared at the ceiling. "This is a fine mess."

Maddie came to the lodge to negotiate the purchase of the manuscript. If Tony—his old college crush reawakened—hadn't been so het up about spending time with her, she wouldn't be lying in that room with a broken ankle and he might already have a sizeable check to deposit into his dwindling checking account. If only he'd kept his head out of the clouds and his thoughts on business.

But Maddie always did have a crazy effect on him. They probably hadn't exchanged more than a few dozen words in those years at BSU. And yet he'd fallen for her. Hard.

"I must be nuts." That was the only explanation for the old feelings stirring back to life the moment Maddie walked into this lodge.

He rose from the chair and left his office, glancing toward the front desk as it came into view. Audrey was nowhere in sight. Maybe she was in with the patient. Quick strides carried him down the hall to the guestroom. He hesitated a moment, then rapped on the door.

Maddie answered, "Yes?"

"It's Tony. May I come in?"

There was a brief silence, then, "Yes."

He turned the knob and opened the door.

She was sitting up in bed, her back propped with pillows. Two more pillows were tucked beneath her right leg. She wore a pink sweatshirt and a pair of black warm-up pants with the right pant leg cut off at the knee. Her ebony hair was caught in a ponytail on the top of her head. Although her face seemed pale, he thought there was less pain in her eyes.

"How're you feeling?" He stepped into the room, stopping near the threshold, his hand resting on the doorknob.

"Better, I think."

"You look better."

She smoothed her hair. "I'll bet."

"No, you do. Really."

"Well, if I do, it's because Audrey has taken good care of me."

"She loves to mother people."

"She's been very kind. But I feel like such a bother." She looked at the bottle of narcotics on top of the nightstand. "I don't think I'll take any more of those pain pills. At least not during the day. They really knock me for a loop. I can't stay awake, let alone think straight."

"You probably needed to sleep. Your body's mending. How's the pain?"

"Bearable."

"Is there anything I can get for you?"

"No. I have everything I need. Would I be in anyone's way if I moved to the reading room for a while? It might be more pleasant to work out there than in here."

He let his gaze move over the guestroom—the dark

paneled walls, the worn forest-green carpet, the single window that faced the storage shed. "Sorry about the dismal accommodations. It seemed better to have you on the ground floor."

"I didn't mean to sound like I was complaining about the room. Please don't apologize." She blushed as she lowered her eyes. "It would be awful if Audrey had to climb the stairs to wait on me." She looked up again. "In fact, that should stop altogether. I know she has other things to do."

Tony thought that extra color in her cheeks was most becoming. She looked lovely. Sweet. Vulnerable. Kissable.

Ker-thump.

Kissable?

Easy there, Anderson.

He decided now would be a good time to leave. Clearing his throat, he pointed at the crutches leaning against the wall near the head of the bed. "Can you manage those all right?"

"Yes, I can manage."

"Okay then. I'll leave you in peace." He gave an abrupt nod and slipped out of the room.

Kissable, indeed.

Ker-thump.

The moment the door closed, Maddie covered her face with her hands. Did she look as flushed as she felt? Oh, she hoped not. Schoolgirls blushed, not career-focused businesswomen.

But she feared the worst. Her skin was warm to the

touch. And why? Because, right in the middle of telling Tony she wanted to work in the reading room, she'd noticed how handsome he looked in his plaid flannel shirt, blue jeans and work boots. And then she'd thought how small the room felt with him standing in it. Small and…intimate.

Oh, my. Those pain pills had done more than make her sleepy. They'd made her lose all common sense.

Moving with care, she lowered her legs over the side of the bed, grimacing as the throbbing in her broken ankle intensified. Yet it was bearable, as she'd told Tony.

Tony… Could he possibly be the same guy she remembered from college? Glasses. Kind of skinny and very quiet. Smart but shy. Maybe her memory was flawed. Maybe she was thinking of someone else.

Which, of course, didn't matter in the least. It wasn't some college kid who wanted to sell a collectible manuscript to David. It was a businessman who needed cash flow.

"Back to business, Maddie," she whispered as she reached for her crutches.

It took longer than she anticipated to wash up in the bathroom. There wasn't much she could do with her hair except leave it in a ponytail. However, she wasn't leaving this room without mascara and lipstick. She didn't want to frighten the other guests.

She chose a dark brown sweater from her clothes in the dresser, but she didn't change out of the warm-up pants. She wasn't willing to cut off a leg from any of the trousers or jeans she'd brought with her from California. Not unless she was forced to.

Ready at last, she slipped the strap of her computer case over her shoulder and, leaning on the crutches, made her way out of the guestroom, down the hall and into the lobby.

Audrey Tremaine was behind the front desk, speaking to someone on the telephone. Her eyes widened when she saw Maddie.

Maddie released the grip on her right crutch and pleasantly waved Audrey off before she continued across the lobby. In the reading room, a fire crackled on the hearth and the scent of pine garlands filled the air. Christmas lights twinkled around the frames of the windows and across the fireplace mantel. Outside the sky was a crisp and cloudless blue, sunlight making the snow sparkle.

How beautiful! The light from the windows and the warmth of the room were like a caress. She felt ten times better than she had five minutes before.

After a quick perusal of the room, she chose an overstuffed chair near a north-facing window. A nearby wall socket would provide electricity for her laptop and she wouldn't get as much glare on the computer screen as she might have in one of the other chairs.

She set the computer case on a coffee table, then sank onto the chair and laid her crutches on the floor. The throbbing in her right foot reminded her that she needed to elevate it.

As if summoned, Audrey appeared in the doorway. "Goodness gracious. Are you sure you should be moving about this soon? And, more importantly, is there anything you need?" She bustled into the room.

"I'm sure." Maddie glanced toward the loveseat against the opposite wall. "Come to think of it, I could use a pillow for under my foot. That way I won't worry about scratching the coffee table with this boot."

Audrey fetched two throw pillows from the loveseat and brought them to Maddie. "Here. Let me help you." She moved the computer case to the floor, replacing it with the pillows, then lifted and placed Maddie's right leg atop them. Next she drew a side table away from the wall and positioned it next to Maddie's chair. "How about a nice cup of tea? And don't tell me it'll be too much trouble, because it won't be."

She smiled. "Tea would be lovely. Thank you."

The moment the housekeeper left the room, Maddie drew a deep breath, letting it out slowly. The throbbing in her ankle had worsened over the past few minutes. No surprise, she supposed. She hadn't been up much since her fall.

She leaned her head against the back of the chair and closed her eyes, drawing another deep breath. There. It wasn't so bad now. She would simply relax for a short while, then she would be ready to attend to some work.

The assigned ring of her cell phone announced a call from her mother. Oh, no. What would she tell Mom? She could imagine Doris Scott's reaction. Her mom would want to fly out to take care of her. She wouldn't care that the break was minor or that Maddie could manage fine on her crutches.

Better not to mention it.

She flipped open the phone. "Hi, Mom."

"Hello, dear. How are you enjoying your visit to Idaho?"

"There's lots of snow." That seemed like something safe to say.

"Have you done anything fun?"

"I'm here on business, Mom. Remember?"

"Oh, I know. But I was hoping that you would have a good time. You never seem to do anything fun for yourself."

She swallowed a sigh, wishing her mother didn't worry about her so much.

As if she'd heard Maddie's thoughts, her mom said, "I just want you to be happy, dear. That's all."

"I know. And I love you for it. But I'm okay." Apart from a broken ankle and some persistent self-pity. "I love doing what I do."

For the next few minutes, they talked about Kate and Don and their two kids and everyone's plans for Christmas. Then, fearing the spotlight might return to her—and worse, that she might be forced to tell her mom about her broken ankle—Maddie decided it was time to end the call.

"I'd better get back to work, Mom. I'll call you after I return to L.A. Give my love to everyone."

"I will, dear. You take care. We love you, too."

Flipping the phone closed, Maddie looked out the window. From here, she could see the main ski lift, seats rocking and swaying as they headed skyward. If she hadn't gotten on that silly thing, she wouldn't have to be afraid to talk to her mother. If she had stayed in the lodge where she belonged, she wouldn't—

Right then, Tony appeared outside the window. He carried an ax against his right shoulder as he walked with long strides toward a large tree stump that poked up from the snow. Once there, he swung the ax downward, cutting into the surface of the stump. A nearby wood pile explained his intent.

Maddie leaned to one side for a better view as Tony set to work, chopping large chunks of wood into fireplace-sized pieces. He swung the ax in a smooth arc and the air *cracked* as the blade bit into the logs. Then he jerked the ax free and repeated the cycle. He made the work look easy. He even seemed to enjoy himself.

And she enjoyed watching. Enjoyed just looking at him. A man in his element. What woman wouldn't like to watch him?

She squeezed her eyes closed, alarmed by her wayward thoughts. The last man she'd enjoyed watching as he worked broke her heart into a million tiny pieces.

Not all men cheat on their wives.

No, but some of them did. And if Craig could fool her into thinking he loved her and would cherish her and be faithful to her, why couldn't the next guy fool her, too?

She didn't even want a "next guy." One mistake was enough.

Maddie hated being divorced. Everything in her had longed for a lasting, God-centered marriage, to be one half of a couple who would grow old together. When she pledged herself to Craig, she thought they shared a belief in commitment and fidelity. How could she have *not* known the type of man he was? How could she have been so naive, so blind to the truth?

Because I chose to be.

She never wanted to make the same mistake again.

"It's been almost four years, Maddie," a friend had said to her a month ago. *"It's time for you to get back in the game."* Her response was what it had always been: *"Not interested."*

She opened her eyes and stared out the window, her gaze alighting on Tony.

Jerk. Swing. *Crack.*

Jerk. Swing. *Crack.*

Heaven help me. She needed to conclude her business and get out of there.

Chapter Six

Tony was stacking the last of the chopped wood in the rack outside the back door when two SUVs, a minivan and a Jeep pulled into the lodge parking lot. This had to be the Sullivan family.

He stomped his boots on the mat to make sure he wouldn't track up the clean floors, then opened the door and headed toward the lobby.

"They're here," Audrey announced.

"Yeah, I saw them pull in."

In many ways, the newly-arrived guests—sixteen adults and one toddler—would be a test for Tony and his small staff. The Sullivans, their guests for a full week, would fill the eight rooms in the second story west wing of the lodge. He'd worked like a dog to make sure all was ready for their arrival. The last roll of wallpaper had been hung in the green room late last night.

"I'll go help with the luggage." He glanced at his watch. It was not quite eleven. "Better let Cookie know the Sullivans are here."

"I already did."

"Thanks, Audrey. You're always one step ahead of me."

"Been doing it a long time, is all."

Tony pulled open the front door and stepped onto the porch. With a wave, he called, "Welcome to Cloud Mountain." Then he descended the steps to meet and greet his guests.

It didn't take long to ascertain that the Sullivan clan was a boisterous bunch. The patriarch was Sam Sullivan, newly-retired from the construction business at the age of sixty-eight. Karen, his wife, was short and round with a mischievous sparkle in her green eyes.

The second generation of Sullivan men and their wives all looked to be in their forties. Mike, Roger and Kip Sullivan took after their father in height, looks and build.

The five members of the third generation were more diverse. Somewhere between their late teens and mid-twenties, there were three granddaughters—two of them with husbands, one of those with a red-haired child in arms—and two grandsons, one of them married, his college-aged brother single.

When the introductions were finished, the Sullivans emptied the backs of their four vehicles of numerous suitcases and tote bags, plus sixteen pairs of skis and boots and three ski boards.

Tony grabbed four suitcases and led the way inside. Something told him the lodge was going to feel much smaller with this family as guests.

Maddie was awakened by a commotion in the lobby—and was none too happy about it. She'd been dreaming something delightful, although she couldn't remember what. It had vanished the instant she awoke. She wished she could bring it back.

Straightening in the chair, she moved her laptop to the coffee table. Her arms felt sluggish, as did her mind.

A burst of raucous laughter caused her to start. Who on earth was making all that racket?

Just then a little girl, perhaps a year or so old, toddled into view. She hesitated when she saw Maddie. Her eyes widened, then she squealed in delight and hurried forward, every unsteady step looking as if it would be the last before she fell.

"Iris," a deep male voice called. "Come back here."

The toddler giggled in response. Obviously she had no intention of answering the summons.

"Iris, you heard me. Listen to Daddy."

A fair-haired man appeared in the doorway at the same moment the child arrived at Maddie's chair and hid her face against Maddie's right thigh.

"I'm sorry," the fellow said. "Iris doesn't meet any strangers. She thinks everyone is a friend."

"It's all right." Maddie ran her hand over the little girl's soft wispy curls.

The young father crossed the room in a few strides, captured Iris around the waist and whisked her into the air. She squealed and laughed again as her dad pressed his lips into the curve of her neck and shoulder and blew.

Maddie felt a pinch in her heart, a longing so strong it stole her breath away.

If only...

As if to torture herself, she recalled the tabloid photo— Craig and Shari, joyously awaiting the birth of their child.

If only…

"Did you do that on the ski slopes?"

Pulled from her unhappy thoughts, she wasn't sure what Iris's dad meant.

He pointed at her propped leg. "Did you break something skiing?"

It was Tony who answered. "Actually, she was fine while skiing. It was the falling that got her into trouble." He grinned at Maddie as he entered the room. Turning toward the other man, he said, "Your wife's headed up to your room."

"I'd best get a move on then." He nodded at Maddie. "See you around."

"Yes." She waved at the little girl. "Bye, Iris."

The child waved back.

Tony said, "Cute kid."

"Adorable." Sorrow tightened her throat once again, sorrow for the might-have-been wishes.

"Hope she didn't disturb your work."

"I wasn't getting much done anyway." She drew a deep breath, determined to stop thinking about what she couldn't have. There were other things that should be on her mind. Completing her business with Tony Anderson, for one. "You know, we should discuss the matter of the manuscript some time today. I need to leave soon and—"

"You're not supposed to drive with that broken ankle. Remember?"

"Don't worry. I'll work out some way to get home.

But in the meantime…" Realizing that rushing back to Los Angeles didn't sound as good as it should, she let the sentence drift into silence.

"In the meantime, it's down to business," Tony finished for her.

"Yes."

He checked his watch. "How about three o'clock in my office?"

"I'll be ready."

"Okay." He motioned toward the table near her elbow. "Do you need anything? More tea or maybe some hot chocolate."

"Thank you, but I'm fine. I'll wait for lunch."

With a nod, Tony left the room.

Maddie turned her head to look out the window as tears pooled in her eyes and loneliness coiled around her heart. She would close this deal and head home, but no one would be waiting for her when she got there.

If only…

Stop it. Stop feeling sorry for yourself.

She had much to be thankful for. God had walked her through each stage of grief that followed the death of her marriage. By His grace, she'd come to understand that, while God hated divorce, He did not hate the divorced. He did not hate her. He loved her. He'd collected her tears in a bottle, as the psalm said, and recorded each one in His book. He knew her sorrows and wanted to heal them completely.

Then why don't you trust Him with your future?

Chapter Seven

Maddie's quiet meal with Tony, Audrey and Cookie on the day she arrived stood in stark contrast to today's lunch.

Like the youngest member of their clan, the Sullivans knew no strangers. They treated Maddie like a long-lost member of the family and included her in their conversations as they passed serving bowls around the table.

"Doug broke his leg skiing," Hannah Sullivan said. "When was that, Doug? Four years ago?"

"Five years, Mom. I was a junior in high school."

His brother, Eric, jabbed Doug in the shoulder. "I'll bet Maddie wasn't doing something stupid the way you were."

"Shut up, bonehead."

"Loser."

"Poser."

Some fraternal shoving ensued.

"I apologize, Maddie," Mike Sullivan, their dad, said. "They've been shut up in the car for too many hours. We need to get them fed and out on the slopes where they can burn up some of that energy."

"They don't bother me."

The truth was, it was more bothersome seeing all the happily married couples seated around the tables. Seeing the way Sam deferred to his wife. Watching the tender exchanges between Iris's parents. Hearing Mike's laughter when Hannah told a joke.

Three generations of happy marriages—and her. She felt like a fifth wheel.

"Are you here alone?" Karen Sullivan asked.

Maddie nodded. "Yes."

"What made you choose Cloud Mountain for a solo vacation?" This question came from Iris's father, Wayne Gruber.

Maddie's head ached. "Actually, it's not a vacation." She rubbed the pressure point between her eyebrows. "I'm here on business." *And if I'd remembered that, I wouldn't have a broken ankle.*

Audrey entered the dining room and walked over to Maddie, leaned down and whispered into her ear. "There's someone here to see you."

Maddie drew back so she could look the woman in the eyes. "To see *me*?"

Audrey nodded, then turned her head. Maddie followed her gaze to find David Fairchild standing in the dining room entrance.

"David?"

He moved toward her.

"What are you doing here?" She lowered her leg to

the floor and, bracing herself on the edge of the table, began to rise.

David's hand on her right shoulder gently pushed her back onto her chair. "I came to see how you're doing. Lois and I were worried. You didn't sound like yourself when you called."

Maddie wanted to crawl into a hole and pull the earth over her. "I'm fine, David. It isn't anything serious."

Wasn't it bad enough that she hadn't yet begun negotiations with Tony? Now her employer had made a special trip from California to make sure she was okay. Or worse. Maybe he didn't trust her to close the deal. What had she said to him over the phone when she was in that drug-induced haze? It must be something awful if it made him fly to Idaho in the corporate jet.

Shoot me now!

"Mr. Fairchild." Tony appeared at her left elbow. "I'm Tony Anderson. Welcome to Cloud Mountain Lodge."

Maddie swallowed a groan as the two men shook hands about twelve inches in front of her face.

"It's a pleasure to meet you, Mr. Anderson."

"The pleasure's mine. Will you join us for lunch?"

"Thank you. I'd appreciate it."

Tony motioned toward the smaller table where he'd been seated a few moments before. "There's an empty spot over here."

David patted Maddie's shoulder. "We'll talk after lunch."

She nodded, forcing herself to smile.

As soon as David moved away, Ann Gruber asked, "Is that your father?"

"No." Oh, that miserable, sinking feeling in the pit of her stomach. "He's my boss."

Tony tried not to be obvious as he sized up the millionaire. Despite his steel-gray hair, David looked a good ten years younger than his age. Moreover, he had an air of confidence that was not uncommon in men of power and wealth.

Before Tony turned his back on a management career in the corporate world, he'd known a number of men much like Fairchild—successful, empire-building men with the Midas touch. And some of them were the most miserable human beings a man would ever hope to meet.

Something about David Fairchild said he wasn't miserable. He wore contentment as easily as Tony wore a pair of Levi's and work boots.

"I hope you're planning to stay with us for a day or two." He passed a bowl of mixed vegetables to David.

"Well, at least overnight. Assuming you have a room available."

"We do."

David glanced toward Maddie. "How is she?"

"Better today. The break isn't bad. The doctor says it should mend without a problem, as long as she takes care not to walk on it too soon."

"I'll make certain of that."

Tony wasn't sure he cared for the proprietary note in David's voice. Was there more to his relationship with Maddie than being her employer? He frowned, not liking his train of thought.

He'd done a fair share of research on David Fairchild after receiving word of his interest in buying the Small manuscript. One thing Tony had learned was that David and his wife, Lois, had been married for thirty-one years. By all reports, it was a good marriage. Others looked up to David Fairchild, speaking of him as a man of integrity, a natural leader, someone with a strong personal faith. He didn't seem the type who would be unfaithful to his wife or who would take advantage of a woman young enough to be his daughter.

"Maddie says she knew you in college."

Drawn from his thoughts, Tony answered, "We didn't know each other well, but yes, we were at BSU at the same time."

"I've tried to talk her into going back to school to finish her degree. She doesn't lack many credits." David shook his head slowly. "It's a shame she married Houston. He wasn't good to her."

"You know Craig?"

"I know him." The dark tone of his voice spoke volumes.

And Tony liked him for it.

Maddie was thankful when the meal ended. She smiled and waved at the Sullivans as they emptied out of the dining room, still talking and laughing as they had throughout the meal. Unless she'd misunderstood, they were all headed for the ski slopes, with the exception of Iris and her great-grandmother, who were both going to lie down for a nap. Maddie wouldn't have minded a rest herself, but that wasn't possible now.

She saw Tony rise from the table and bid David a good afternoon. Then he nodded in Maddie's direction before leaving.

"Pleasant fellow." David walked to Maddie's table. "I enjoyed our visit. He said you're meeting with him at three."

"Yes." She drew a quick breath and let it out. "Would you like to join us?"

"No. I believe you'll do better without me."

Maddie hoped the surprise didn't show on her face. She'd been certain he came to the lodge because he thought she would blow the deal. She should have known better. It wasn't David's style.

He sat in the chair next to her. "I've taken a room for the night and will head back tomorrow, unless you need me for something."

"If it weren't for my rental car, I'd plan to go with you. Maybe I could arrange for someone to—"

"No, Maddie. I want you to stay here until the doctor releases you. Enjoy yourself. Remember? Do something fun. Relax. Make a vacation of it."

"Not much fun I can have with this." She motioned toward her foot, propped on the chair to her right.

David stood. "You might be surprised." He grinned. "Now, I imagine you need to prepare for your meeting with Tony and I'd like to take a stroll around Cloud Mountain. Maybe I'll try out the slopes for myself."

"Don't break anything."

He chuckled. "I promise." With a wave of his hand

and a "See you later," he turned and strode out of the dining room.

Maddie shook her head. Could this business trip get any stranger?

Chapter Eight

Tony had most of the clutter cleared off his desk by the time Maddie rapped on the jamb of his office doorway.

"Are you ready for me?"

He stood. "Yes. Please come in." He motioned to a chair in front of his desk. "I've got a stool for you to rest your foot on."

"That was thoughtful. Thank you."

As Maddie maneuvered herself into position with her crutches, Tony rounded the desk and took her briefcase from her, setting it on the floor beside her chair. Then he stepped over to the door and closed it.

"I told Audrey to hold any calls so we won't be interrupted." He returned to his chair and sat down.

"I don't expect this meeting will take long." Maddie opened the file folder she'd taken from her briefcase. "As you know, Mr. Fairchild has verified the authentication of the Uriah Small manuscript. Based upon his research into fair market value, he is prepared to make the following offer." She handed him a piece of paper.

Tony's heart started to race as he looked at the figure.

Two hundred thousand dollars. And that was the starting point. He knew enough about negotiating to know that you never open with your top offer.

But even if the offer went no higher, this would allow him to put a new roof on the lodge before next winter. He could update the plumbing in the west wing. And the kitchen. There ought to be enough for them to start remodeling the kitchen, too. Wait until Cookie heard the news!

Tony leaned back in his chair, hoping his excitement didn't show on his face. "I was wondering. What does Mr. Fairchild intend to do with the manuscript, if it's his?"

"He'll see that it's published. He knows he isn't the only fan of Small's writing and doesn't want to keep it to himself. It should be released so others can enjoy. But the original manuscript will be preserved in his private collection."

"Does he have a large number of collectible manuscripts?"

Maddie's demeanor was all business, her reply measured. "David collects many things. His interests are eclectic. This will be the first manuscript he's acquired."

Tony liked it better when she wasn't so businesslike. "Tell me something. How did you happen to go to work for him?"

"I'm not sure what that has to do with—"

He leaned forward, resting his forearms on the desk. "Humor me."

She watched him in silence, trying to figure out what would bring about the best results for her employer.

Tony offered a slow smile. "I'm curious, Maddie." He could have added *to know more about you.* That's what he wanted—to know more about Maddie Scott. To know everything about her.

A touch of color painted the apples of her cheeks before she lowered her gaze to the folder on her lap. Perhaps he wasn't as good as he thought at disguising his feelings. Maybe he didn't even want to be good at it.

Talk to me. Tell me about yourself, Maddie.

She looked up, her gaze softened. "David and Lois befriended me not long after we moved to Los Angeles. They could tell I was a fish out of water and took pity on me."

"You? A fish out of water?" That was hard to envision. She'd seemed confident in every gathering during college.

"Very much so."

"How did you meet the Fairchilds?"

"David is a good friend of the team's defensive coach, and our paths crossed at different functions."

"And that's when you went to work for him?"

"No." She shook her head. "I wasn't employed while… while Craig and I were married. But after the divorce, I—" She broke off suddenly and again lowered her eyes, but not before he caught the glint of pain.

Was she still in love with her ex-husband?

Maddie drew a deep breath and stiffened her shoulders. "The truth is, David's offer of employment was a godsend. Without a degree or an employment history to fall back on, I had little hope of making much of a living. Certainly not enough to help me pay off my debts."

"Debts?"

"I know what you're thinking." She gave him a self-deprecating smile. "Everyone assumes I received a large settlement in the divorce. However, I wasn't very smart about it. I didn't hire an attorney right away. I was so sure God wouldn't let the divorce go through that I kept procrastinating. I kept thinking Craig would change his mind and all would be well. Denial with a capital *D*. In the end, I agreed to things I shouldn't have. I let myself be tricked by Craig and that shark of a lawyer he hired."

"I'm sorry, Maddie. I didn't mean to bring up bad memories."

"You didn't know."

"It was insensitive to ask."

She was silent for a long moment, then said, "You weren't insensitive, Tony. You've been nothing but kind to me since I arrived."

He'd like to be even more kind, if she'd let him. He'd like to prove that he was the sort of guy who wouldn't hurt her or trick her or coerce her. If she would just give him enough time to prove it.

Tony's gaze made Maddie go all quivery on the inside. There was something sweet and gentle about it. Something that made her want to stay right here in this chair and bask in it.

Which was the very reason she decided it was time to leave.

She reached for her briefcase. "You think about that offer, Tony, and we'll talk again tomorrow, if that's all right with you." She stood.

"Yes. That's a good idea. We'll talk tomorrow afternoon." He rose from his chair, went to the door and opened it for her. "Would you like help with your briefcase?"

"No, thanks. I'm getting the hang of these crutches and the briefcase is light." With scarcely a glance in his direction, she left the office and returned to her guestroom.

What happened back there?

She sank onto the side of the bed and replayed the brief meeting in her mind. It hadn't gone at all as she'd expected it to. Usually she got some sense of a person's reaction to the initial offer. Not so with Tony. She hadn't a clue whether he thought it too low or much higher than expected. What was she going to tell David when he asked how the meeting went? She and Tony hadn't said more than a few words about the offer. Certainly nothing that could be called a negotiation. And how in the world had they arrived at the topic of her divorce and her resulting debt?

She groaned.

"Maybe I can blame it on those stupid pain pills."

Except she hadn't taken one today.

Humor me. She remembered the deep timbre of Tony's voice, the smile that slowly curved the corners of his mouth. *I'm curious, Maddie.* Her stomach fluttered again, as it had when he'd spoken those words in his office. Not good. Definitely not good. She had a job to do, and it didn't include an attraction to the proprietor of the Cloud Mountain Lodge.

She released a sigh. Nothing about this trip was

going as expected. From that lousy tabloid headline to her broken ankle to this less-than-professional start to her negotiations on David's behalf.

Pull yourself together. Now.

Another deep breath. There. She felt better. The next time she met with Tony, she would stay focused on the business at hand.

It didn't take Tony long to find David Fairchild. The man was sitting in the Grounds for Happiness Coffee Shop at the corner of Main and Third, enjoying a tall drink.

"Mind if I join you?"

"Not at all." David waved to the other chair at the table. "Please do."

Tony caught the eye of Nancy, the barista, and nodded. He'd been in here often enough since buying the lodge for her to know what to bring him. He liked his coffee black and strong.

"So what do you think of our little town?" he asked as he sat opposite David.

"Nice. Some interesting shops and the people are friendly. I met one elderly gentleman who knew Uriah Small rather well."

"Walter Hopkins?"

"Yes. He was a font of information about Cloud Mountain in the mid-twentieth century. And about Uriah Small. We had quite a fascinating discussion."

Tony chuckled. "Walt knows a lot about many things. I hope my mind is as sharp when I'm half his age."

"Amen to that." David took a drink from his coffee

cup. "Walter also said he hopes the publicity about the manuscript will bring more tourists here to ski."

"The whole town hopes that." Tony removed the lid from the coffee Nancy brought to the table. Steam rose in a translucent ribbon above the cup. "May I ask you something? About Maddie."

David cocked an eyebrow but said nothing.

"She says you and your wife have been good friends of hers for quite a while."

"Yes."

"So you must know her pretty well. Especially since you two work together now."

"Maddie's like a daughter to us."

Tony could see how that would happen. The Maddie he remembered from their college days had drawn people to her with an easy smile and enchanting laugh. More than once he'd observed her helping someone that other students on campus never noticed needed help. Perhaps it was her genuine kindness that first made him want to know her better. Just because she was part of the "cool crowd" in college, it didn't go to her head.

If not for Craig Houston...

He blew across the coffee in his cup before taking a sip. "I know she got burned in her marriage. Is she over it?" *Is she over him?*

David frowned. "I'm not sure that's any of—"

"I only ask because I care about her...a lot."

Silence stretched between them. Tony knew he was being sized up and hoped he passed muster.

At long last, David said, "I see."

"Just in case you're wondering, this doesn't have anything to do with the manuscript."

"Strangely enough, I believe you." The older man nodded. "And because I believe you, I'll answer your question. Yes, she's over Craig. But the hurt is still there. He left some deep scars."

Tony hadn't liked Craig Houston back in college, but he didn't know if that was because the guy was a jock or a jerk. Maybe both. Either way, Craig had taken Maddie's love and thrown it away. That made him the lowest of life-forms in Tony's book.

He rose from the chair. "Maybe I can do something about those scars." He snapped the lid onto the coffee cup. "At least I'd like to try."

Chapter Nine

"**O**h good. You're here."

Maddie looked up from the paperback novel to see Hannah Sullivan standing in the entry to the reading room, her granddaughter Iris braced on her hip.

"We've signed up our family to go on a sleigh ride tonight. We'd like you to join us."

Maddie laid the book face down on the coffee table next to her foot. The invitation was tempting. She was growing bored with sitting around. She was used to being more active.

Ann Gruber stepped into view to stand next to her mother. "Please come. The guys will make sure you don't hurt your ankle while we're out."

By *the guys*, Maddie assumed Ann meant her husband and two brothers.

"It's a horse-drawn wagon bed on skids with bells, lights and hay bales," Hannah said. "The driver says the route takes about an hour. He'll pick us up here at the lodge at seven and bring us back by eight or so. Ought to be pretty out with the full moon."

"It does sound like fun, but I may need to meet with David when he returns and—"

"Oh, I'm sorry." Hannah laughed. "I should have told you. We saw Mr. Fairchild in town on our way back to the lodge and he's planning to go on the sleigh ride, too."

Maddie felt her eyes go wide. "He is?"

"Yes."

"Well then, I'd love to join you." How could she turn down an opportunity to see the distinguished president and CEO of Fairchild Enterprises sitting on a bale of hay? In fact, she'd better take her camera. Lois would want to see some photos of that.

"Here, Mom." Ann held out her arms. "Give me Iris. I need to change her diaper."

Hannah kissed the toddler on the top of her head before passing the child to Ann. "I'll be up shortly." After her daughter and granddaughter left, Hannah entered the room and sat on the loveseat across from Maddie. "It was lovely on the mountain today. The snow is perfect. Most of the family is still at it. I hope the skiing stays like this the whole time we're here."

"How long will that be?"

"Through next Sunday. It's a Sullivan family tradition. Every third year, we meet somewhere to celebrate an early Christmas together, nine days and eight nights, the whole lot of us. Three years ago, we went to Hawaii, but this year we decided we wanted to enjoy a white Christmas. My father-in-law came to Cloud Mountain to ski years and years ago and stayed in this lodge. He didn't even know if it was still open, so he was excited when he found the website and was able to book us in." Hannah looked around the room. "It's a lovely old place, isn't it?"

"Yes. It has—" Maddie sought for the right word "—character."

"I agree. Mr. Anderson's done an admirable job of modernizing it without sacrificing any of its charm."

Maddie nodded.

"I can see why he wanted to restore it and I admire his courage. It isn't easy to leave what seems safe and secure to pursue your dreams."

"No," Maddie answered softly. "It isn't." I admire him, too. I wish I had some of that same courage.

From outside came the sound of stomping boots mixed with laughter.

"The crew has returned." Hannah rose from the love-seat. "I'd best go hurry my men along or they'll never be ready for supper. See you there."

Maddie listened as the Sullivans left their skis and boots on the porch, then spilled into the lodge and made their way up the stairs to their rooms. A twinge of envy tightened her chest. She'd often wished to be part of a family—large, extended, demonstrative. She used to imagine herself with three or four children, going for a visit to her sister in Florida. All the little cousins running and playing. Laughter and love blended together in perfect harmony.

What a beautiful dream that had been.

More voices intruded on her thoughts—David's and Audrey's, coming from the lobby. She reached for her crutches and got up from the chair, but before she had time to move around the coffee table, David appeared in the doorway.

"Did you hear about the sleigh ride?"

"Yes, I heard. I'm just on my way to my room. I need to decide what to wear." She looked down at her right leg. "This could be a problem."

"It won't be. We'll take along lots of blankets. That'll keep you snug." He crossed the room and draped an arm around her shoulders, giving her a fatherly squeeze. "I'm glad you agreed to go, Maddie. It'll be good for you to do something fun."

"It was doing something fun that got my ankle broken." She rolled her eyes at him. "Besides, I couldn't very well refuse the invitation, since you're going, Lois will want me to tell her all about it. You'll leave out too many details for her satisfaction."

"Ah, you know me well."

"Yes, I do."

David took a step back. "So how did your meeting go with Tony?"

"I'm not sure." She hated admitting what a poor job she'd done at the outset of the negotiations, but there was no way around it. "We…we got sidetracked. Completely my fault." She lifted her chin in a show of confidence. "We're going to talk again tomorrow afternoon and I'll make sure we stay on topic."

Her boss smiled. "I'm not worried. In fact, I don't mind if you give him more time to weigh his options. After all, you won't be leaving on Monday since you can't drive. You can afford to take your talks with Tony a bit slow." He paused a moment and his voice deepened. "I like that young man, Maddie. He has vision and drive. He'll put the money he gets from selling the manuscript to good use."

She couldn't have explained why, not even to herself, but she was pleased by David's approval of Tony. "I'll do my best to make sure he accepts your offer."

"I know you will. Never doubted it for a moment." He took another step back. "I'd better let you check on your wardrobe for the sleigh ride. We can talk about the negotiations before I leave tomorrow. But no thoughts about business tonight."

Tony wouldn't normally join his guests on a sleigh ride, but nothing about life at the lodge was normal at present. Not as long as Maddie was among his guests. So when Hannah Sullivan suggested he come along—and he learned that both Maddie and her boss were going—he was quick to agree.

His first priority was to make sure he got to sit beside Maddie before one of Sam Sullivan's single grandsons got there first. Those boys might be eight to ten years younger than Maddie, but he doubted that would stop them from flirting. He'd already observed some of that over dinner—and hadn't been any too pleased about it, either.

Nick Robertson and his son Randy drove two sleighs into the lodge's parking lot a little before seven o'clock. The sleighs weren't fancy, but the Christmas lights strung from front to back made them look like carriages fit for a princess and the bells on the harnesses chimed a merry tune.

"Do you need help out to the sleigh, Maddie?" Doug Sullivan asked.

Before Maddie could answer, Tony said, "He's right. It isn't a good idea for you to try to walk out there in the snow with those crutches." He took the closest crutch from her and gave it to Doug. "You hold this, and I'll carry Maddie." Then he swept her into his arms. She looked at him with wide eyes and he prayed he hadn't moved too fast for his own good. "Better give Doug that other crutch. It'll make it easier to carry you down the steps."

She complied without looking away.

Man, she had beautiful eyes. Chocolate-brown pools that revealed a hint of vulnerability, a touch of wistfulness. And her mouth… A generous mouth, ripe for kissing.

Ker-thump.

He swallowed hard as he carried her down the porch steps and out to the nearest sleigh. Nick had a step stool waiting at the back of the wagon bed and Tony climbed it, keeping a protective grip on the woman in his arms. With care, he set her on one of the side benches, her back against the outer rail. Then he pulled one of the hay bales close for her to use as a prop for her right leg. All this he accomplished while blocking the way for anyone who might try to sit beside her.

By the time Tony tucked a blanket around Maddie's right leg and took his seat on the bench on her left side, the rest of the group had found their own places in the two sleighs. But he gave little notice to who was where. He only cared that Maddie was by his side.

"Do you go on these sleigh rides often?" she asked, a slight smile bowing the corners of her mouth.

"No, this is a first for me. The last time I took a sleigh ride it was a junior high church event."

"How about you, David?" Maddie turned her gaze to the other side of the wagon. "How many sleigh rides have you been on?"

Her boss chuckled. "Not many opportunities in Los Angeles."

"What about when you and Lois vacation in Aspen?"

"Not yet. Maybe next time we're there." He was quiet a moment, then said, "On second thought, maybe we'll skip Aspen and come to Cloud Mountain. Lois would like it here."

Nick climbed onto the driver's seat and took the reins in hand before tossing over his shoulder, "Here we go, folks. Hold on." He slapped the leather reins against the horses' rumps and the sleigh slid into action.

As if on cue, the moon—full and so large it seemed within reach—rose above the western ridge.

"Oh my." Karen Sullivan pointed. "Isn't it beautiful?"

Everyone in their sleigh looked at the moon. Everyone except Tony. He continued to feast his eyes on Maddie, her face brushed with moonlight.

Beautiful.

Silence fell over them as the sleighs left the town behind. The only sounds were the soft *shooshing* of the skids sliding over the snow-covered trail and the jingle of bells on the harnesses.

Maddie turned her head toward Tony. When their

gazes met, the smile she wore slowly faded until all that was left was the look of vulnerability he'd glimpsed earlier. The breath caught in his chest. It would be easy to lean forward and capture her lips with his own. Would she welcome his kiss or despise him for it?

From the other sleigh came the sound of voices raised in song.

"Silent night, holy night. All is calm, all is bright…"

Soon, those in the sleigh with Tony chimed in.

"Round yon Virgin Mother and Child. Holy infant so tender and mild."

Maddie's voice was soft but crystal clear. It seemed to wrap around Tony's heart and squeeze it.

Is it crazy to feel the way I do? She's only been here a few days and yet…

"Sleep in heavenly peace. Sleep in heavenly peace…"

And yet I can't stand the thought of her not being here. Lord, is it possible she might want to stay?

One Christmas carol led to another and another and another. The music seemed to belong in the forest, rising above the sleighs, swallowed by the stately pine trees and snowy mountainsides. And with each note Maddie sang, her heart grew lighter.

Hope. That's what she felt. *Hope.*

She cast a surreptitious glance in Tony's direction, not surprised when she found him still watching her. She wished the trees weren't obscuring the moonlight just now. She would like to see what was behind his unswerving gaze.

But perhaps she knew already. She'd seen several

emotions in the depths of his eyes earlier—attraction, tenderness, kindness. He seemed a solid sort of man, one whose feelings were steady and sure.

Why do I think that's true about you? I've known you such a short while.

"Don't stop singing," he said softly. "You've got a nice voice."

"Do I?"

"Yes."

Despite the chill in the night air, her cheeks grew warm, making her thankful for the darkness.

"I was wondering." He leaned closer. "Would you like to go to church with me in the morning?"

He was so close, she felt the warmth of his breath on her cheek, making it hard to focus on his words. What was it he'd asked her? Something about church. Oh, yes. Did she want to go to church with him?

"I think you'd like it there," he added. "It's a small congregation, but the preacher knows how to teach the Word and the choir is pretty good, too."

She couldn't recall receiving a nicer invitation in years. Maybe not ever. She'd been asked to attend movie premieres and art exhibits, the opera and the ballet. While still married to Craig, she'd been a guest at countless parties in houses the size of some palaces, surrounded by women dripping with diamonds. But nothing sounded as pleasant as going to church with Tony Anderson.

"What do you say?"

She drew a quick breath and answered, "Yes."

His smile widened as he drew back a few inches.

"Great." Then, as if it were the most natural thing in the world, he rested his right arm on the rail behind her back.

Maddie's heart thrummed as a pleasant warmth spread through her veins. How easy it would be to lean against him. How nice it would be to trust again.

If only she could.

Chapter Ten

Fortunately for Maddie, she'd packed two business suits, one of which had a skirt. Wearing a skirt to church would mean she didn't have to cut a leg off a pair of her good slacks, something she was loath to do.

Somehow she managed to bathe and dress on Sunday morning without injuring another part of her anatomy in the process. Then, as satisfied as she could be with her appearance, she hobbled into the dining room just as the Sullivans were finding places at the tables. David was there, too, and when he saw her, he pulled out the chair next to him and motioned for her to be seated.

"How did you rest?" he asked as she drew near.

"Like a rock. All that smog-free night air did me good. I didn't even need a pain pill."

David nodded. "Glad to hear it." He took her crutches and set them against the wall. "You look nice. I understand you're going to church with Tony."

"Yes. Will you join us?"

"Wish I could, but I'd best hit the road after breakfast. I told the pilot I'd be at the airport by eleven."

She straightened on her chair. "But we were going to talk about the negotiations before I meet with Tony again."

"I gave that some thought and I don't think it's necessary." He took the cloth napkin from beside his plate and spread it open on his lap. "Maddie, you know what to do. You're good at it."

Yes, she knew what to do. She was a competent negotiator in ordinary circumstances. But doing business with Tony didn't feel ordinary.

David leaned closer. "Trust your instincts."

"Easy for you to say."

"I have confidence in you."

She wished she could say the same about herself, but she couldn't. Everything about this trip seemed off-kilter. First there'd been that headline about Craig and Shari and their pregnancy. Then there'd been her broken ankle, something that never would have happened if she'd kept her mind on business. And now? Now there were these...*feelings* about Tony, feelings that had nothing to do with negotiating the purchase of the Uriah Small manuscript for David's collection, nothing to do with closing the deal so that she could collect her commission and pay off her debts. Feelings she could ill afford to entertain.

Not now.

It wasn't worth the risk.

Redeemer Community Church looked like something off a Currier & Ives Christmas card: wood siding painted white; long and narrow with plenty of windows;

a tall steeple; snow piled high all around it; mountains rising majestically in the background; pine wreaths with red bows decorating each of the double doors at the entrance.

As Maddie climbed the steps, she felt Tony's gentle touch on the small of her back, a gesture of support, a silent message that he wouldn't allow her to fall. Emotion tightened her throat. She didn't want to be so moved by his unspoken concern, but she was.

"Maddie, this is Luke Matthews, our pastor. Luke, I'd like you to meet Maddie Scott."

Tony's words of introduction pulled her attention to the man standing inside the doorway. She smiled as she took the minister's proffered hand.

"Glad you could join us today, Miss Scott."

"Thank you."

The pastor cast his gaze downward at the red boot on her right leg. "Did our mountain do that to you?"

"Yes."

"I hope you'll forgive us." Luke looked dutifully remorseful.

Maddie laughed. "I believe I will."

She and Tony moved through the narthex, stopping several times for Tony to make more introductions. The small sanctuary was exactly as she imagined every country church should look—scuffed hardwood floor, wooden pews with faded red seat cushions, a choir loft big enough for ten people at most, an upright piano on the right side, a raised pulpit on the left.

Tony stopped beside the third pew from the front

and waited until she was settled, her crutches beneath the pew in front of her, before he sat down beside her.

Softly, she said, "I feel like I've stepped into the church in that old Disney movie *Pollyanna*. Don't you think so?"

"Sorry. Never saw it." In contrast to the ordinary words of response, his voice was low and intimate. "Not exactly a boy's kind of movie."

She felt heat rise to her cheeks. "No, I suppose not."

"A favorite movie of yours?"

"No, but I've seen it lots of times. My mom owns the DVD. She loves it." Maddie was babbling now but couldn't seem to help herself. "She'd love this church, too."

"How about your church in L.A? What's it like?"

"Very different from this." She looked away, once more allowing her gaze to travel around the room, taking in the stained-glass window and the lifesized wooden cross. "Very different."

"Is it a big church?"

"Yes. About ten thousand members."

"Must be many opportunities to serve in a church that size."

Chords from the piano ended their conversation and Maddie was thankful. Tony's last comment had struck a nerve. Over the past few years, she had been less and less active in her church. She blamed it on work and frequent travel. But those were only excuses.

As the congregation stood, Maddie listened to Tony's voice raised in song and knew, deep in her heart, that he wasn't the sort of man to offer excuses. She suspected he was deeply involved in this small church and with the people of his community.

And she envied him.

Pastor Luke, preaching a series on the fruit of the Spirit, was in great form that morning.

Thanks, Lord.

Tony couldn't help it. He'd wanted Maddie to hear a good sermon, one that would show that this church might be small but it embraced truth and the Author of truth.

Is that pride on my part, Father?

Maybe so, but he thought not. Redeemer Community was a boon to everyone in the area, not only to those who attended services here. When there was a need, its members were the first to show up and the last to leave. In the almost eight months he'd lived in Cloud Mountain, he'd seen this church in action and it was one more reason he knew he'd made the right decision in moving to Idaho and buying the lodge.

Would any of that be enough to make Maddie want to settle here? And as much as he'd like to deny it—not being the sort of man who fell in love at first sight— having Maddie stay in Cloud Mountain was what he wanted. He wanted her with him. He wanted to love her and care for her, to laugh with her and cry with her.

I can't explain why I feel the way I do about her, God. Could this be Your doing? You had to know it was Maddie who would come to negotiate for the manuscript. You had to know her being here would stir up all those old memories and lots of new feelings. Is it Your will that she stay? Is it Your will that I love her?

He hoped so. Because as much as he wanted Maddie with him, he wanted God's will more.

Help me to know what Your will is, Father.

The Sullivan clan—with the exception of Sam, Karen and Iris—had left for the ski slopes before Maddie and Tony returned to the lodge. It made for a more serene Sunday dinner for those who remained behind. The conversation around the table flowed easily from one topic to another, from construction to the stock market, from the fall movie season to the latest hot novels being touted by the talking heads, from the current snow pack to the advantages of all-wheel-drive vehicles.

Maddie enjoyed every moment, but her favorite part was when Sam Sullivan asked Tony to tell them about his decision to leave the corporate world, return to Idaho and restore this old lodge. She loved seeing the way excitement lit his eyes as he answered the question. There was no mistaking his love for this town or his aspirations for the lodge.

She wanted to see those aspirations come to fruition. She wanted him to achieve his dreams. And the best way to do that was to close the deal on the manuscript so he had the necessary working capital. But closing the deal would also mean it was time for her to go back to L.A, and, strangely enough, she wasn't ready to leave.

When had that changed?

Karen Sullivan stood, pulling Maddie from her private thoughts.

"It's time I put this little one and myself down for a nap. What about you, Grandpa? Care to join us?"

"Can't," her husband answered. "I've challenged Cookie to a game of chess."

From the kitchen, Cookie called, "He may wish he'd chosen that nap by the time I've whupped him."

Everyone laughed.

With the meal at an end, Audrey bid everyone a pleasant day before leaving to visit a friend for the afternoon. Tony rose from his chair and began clearing dishes from the table. Karen disappeared up the stairs with Iris in her arms while Sam headed for the reading room to set up the chessboard. Within minutes, everyone but Maddie was gone from the dining room.

She felt at loose ends. She could go to her room and take a nap like Karen and Iris or she could get her book to read or she could open her laptop and go over some business items. Only she didn't want to. She wanted to stay with Tony.

She grabbed her crutches and made her way to the kitchen. Pushing the swinging door open before her, she asked, "Would you like some help with the dishes? I could dry."

Tony glanced over his shoulder, then turned off the running water. "I'm sorry. What did you say?"

"I offered to help, if you'd like."

"No thanks. Guests of the lodge aren't required to wash their dishes." He grinned. "We're laid-back, but not that laid-back. Unless, of course, you can't pay your bill. Then we might have to put you to work."

"I'm not a paying guest." She entered the kitchen and

the door swung closed behind her. "My room is complimentary. Remember?"

"True." His eyes narrowed as he looked at her. "But I bet you should rest and keep that foot up."

"I'm fine. It's not hurting at all." Okay, that was a slight fib. There was some discomfort, but nothing to make a fuss over.

Tony held up a dishtowel. "All right. If you're sure."

"I'm sure." She maneuvered her way around the center island to the right side of the sink. "I wanted to thank you for inviting me to church. I loved the service and your pastor is wonderful."

"Yeah, we're blessed to have Luke leading our congregation. I think his teaching is anointed. Dozens of churches would want to hire him in a second if he decided to leave Cloud Mountain."

"There were times this morning when I felt as if he was speaking just to me."

Tony smiled. "It's great when the Holy Spirit does that, isn't it?"

"Yes."

But I haven't felt that way in a long time. Have I been keeping God at arm's length? Have I closed my ears to His Spirit?

Maddie wasn't ready to explore those questions, so she asked another of Tony. "Where's Cookie?"

"He went to change his clothes before the big chess match. He doesn't find a willing victim very often."

"He's good?"

Tony nodded. "He's *good*."

Maddie set the crutches aside and leaned her hip

against the counter, dishtowel ready. "You three are like family, aren't you? You and Audrey and Cookie."

"Yeah, we are. I might own the place, but they want it to succeed as much as I do."

"I know Cookie lives here in the lodge, but what about Audrey?"

"She has her own house about a quarter mile down the road." As he talked, Tony filled the sink with hot water, the dish soap piling high above the surface. "She stays overnight here when she needs to, but that doesn't happen often. Eventually, we'll hire more full-time help. God willing, the day we need more help will come soon."

Selling the manuscript will help you make it happen. David wants it and is willing to pay. We could close the deal this afternoon.

Tony placed some dirty dishes in the sink and soap bubbles flew into the air in small clusters. One bunch landed on Maddie's nose. Before she could brush at it with her hand, Tony leaned toward her and blew the bubbles away.

Her breathing slowed. Her heartbeat doubled. She felt lightheaded.

Tony took the dishtowel from her, dried his hands, then clasped her shoulders, as if afraid she might crumple to the floor. Only that wasn't why his hands gripped her arms.

He held her as a prelude to a kiss.

His lips were warm, the pressure light and tender. He smelled of a musky cologne and wood smoke. The two combined made for a heady, masculine scent. She closed her eyes and breathed it in.

All too soon, Tony drew back, ending the kiss. She looked at him and saw questions in his eyes, questions for which she had no answers. She only knew she wanted him to kiss her again, to go on kissing her.

Don't stop. Don't stop.

Tony cleared his throat and drew back a little further. "Maybe we'd better get these dishes washed."

It felt like a rejection. Perhaps it shouldn't, but it did.

"Yes," she whispered. "I guess we should."

"Maddie…"

She looked down at her hands. "Let's not talk about it, Tony. It's better we stick to business. Don't you think?"

He didn't reply.

That was answer enough for Maddie.

Chapter Eleven

He shouldn't have kissed her. It was too soon. He'd moved too fast.

Okay, so he'd had a crush on her a decade ago. A crush so strong he even remembered she liked hot tea with milk instead of lemon. But it wasn't as if they'd dated. She hadn't known him from Adam. Not really. Not until a few days ago.

And even if she *did* know him from Adam now, what future was there for the two of them? She lived in L.A. He lived in Cloud Mountain. If two more different places existed in America, he didn't know what they were. La-la-land and the backwoods. Why would he think she'd want to live here? And there was no way he wanted to return to a big city.

But if he made the improvements in the lodge, if their ski resort could begin competing with some of the others in Idaho, if…

If…if…if…

Maddie finished drying the dishes, but Tony could tell she no longer wanted to be there. As soon as the last pot was done, she excused herself and beat a hasty retreat.

Why was I so stupid? Why didn't I keep my head?

Because he loved her.

There. It was that simple. He loved her. Maybe it didn't make sense. Maybe it had happened too fast. But that's how he felt. He loved her.

With his palms pressed against the counter, he bowed his head. *Lord, help me out here. I'm confused and I don't know what to do next.*

He waited. Waited for God's voice to speak to his heart. Waited for a flash of inspiration. Waited to be overwhelmed by the knowledge of what he should say or do. He waited, but none of those things happened.

He wished life as a Christian were sometimes easier. There were many things spelled out in the Bible, but who to love, who to marry, wasn't one of them. There was no verse that said, "Tony Anderson, Maddie Scott is the girl for you." Be nice if there were.

He opened his eyes and looked out the window. It was snowing. The forecast had said they could get from six to ten inches before tomorrow morning. It looked like the weatherman got it right this time.

After a quick glance around the kitchen to make sure all was as it should be—lest he get on Cookie's bad side—he headed for the reading room to see how the chess match was going. If Cookie didn't win, they'd *all* be on his bad side for the next couple of days.

He stopped at the entrance to the room, unnoticed by either of the older men. Both Sam and Cookie stared at the chessboard, frowns of concentration furrowing their brows.

Better not disturb them, he decided. He turned on his heel and walked to his office where he awakened his computer from sleep mode. A short while later, he scanned the messages in his email inbox, including a number of queries about the lodge and the surrounding area. Couldn't have too many of those. There was also an email from a cousin and some general business correspondence that needed attention. He might as well tackle them all.

An hour later, Tony hit Send on his final reply and leaned back in his chair, stretching his arms over his head to work out the kinks. He supposed now would be a good time to have his meeting with Maddie. Only he wasn't sure—

The phone rang and he reached for it. "Cloud Mountain Lodge."

"Tony. It's Frank Martin."

"Hey, Doc. Calling to check on your patient?" He had his finger poised to send the call through to Maddie's room.

"No. We've got some missing skiers."

Tony straightened. "Who?" The faces of his guests flashed before his eyes. Had something happened to one of the Sullivans?

"Gary Patterson and his girlfriend, Nancy Barrett. They went cross-country skiing with some other young folk this morning. Those two fell behind and never made it to the rendezvous point."

Gary hadn't lived in Cloud Mountain much longer

than Tony, but he was a good skier. Nancy had lived here most of her life and knew her way around these mountains. Both were smart enough to take shelter from the storm if they had to.

"We're organizing a search," Frank added.

He stood. "What do you need from me?"

"There's a couple different ways they might have gone. I'm going with Chuck Barrett to Snake Flats. Can you take your Sno-Cat up the logging road to Frazier Ridge?"

"Of course."

"Meet us at the Dry Creek parking lot. We'll coordinate from there."

"I'm on my way."

Tony dropped the handset into its cradle and turned just as Audrey appeared in the doorway.

"Did you hear about Nancy and Gary?" she asked.

"Yes. I'm headed up to Frazier Ridge in the Sno-Cat."

"I'll put together some blankets and a couple of thermos bottles of hot coffee." Audrey looked at her wristwatch. "You have about three hours of daylight left."

"Is it still snowing?"

"Yes. It's bad out there. I had a dickens of a time getting back to the lodge. Couldn't see much past the hood of the car."

In other words, no time to waste. While Audrey went to the kitchen to prepare the thermoses, Tony headed for his private quarters to change into attire more suitable to blizzard conditions. By the time he returned, Cookie, Sam and Maddie had joined Audrey in the lobby. Karen was there, too, sitting on a wooden chair, holding Iris on her lap.

"Audrey told us what happened," Maddie said. "What can we do to help?"

"Pray. Pray hard."

"Shouldn't someone go with you?" Her eyes were filled with worry.

He shook his head. "No, I'll be okay. I've got a radio in the Cat. I can call for help if I need it." He felt the urge to hug Maddie. He'd love to fold her in his arms and kiss her once before he left.

"I put the thermoses and blankets by the back door," Audrey said. "Don't forget to grab some extra flashlights. Cookie and I will whip up some grub in case any search teams bring the skiers here."

"Thanks, Audrey. Hopefully we'll all be back before nightfall."

Tony hadn't been gone more than ten minutes when footsteps on the front porch drew all eyes toward the door. Moments later, the rest of the Sullivans tromped into the lobby.

"Oh, thank goodness!" Karen dashed into the lobby and began hugging her children and grandchildren, one after another. "I was getting worried. Why didn't you get off that mountain when the storm began?"

Her oldest son, Mike, gave her a puzzled look. "It wasn't all that bad until thirty minutes ago."

Audrey said, "We've got some cross-country skiers lost in the storm. It's made everyone anxious."

"We hadn't heard. Sorry, Mom." Mike put his arm

around Karen's shoulders and gave her a squeeze. "We're all okay. Sorry we worried you."

Maddie went into the reading room, but she was too restless to sit down. Instead she leaned against her crutches while staring out the window. Not that she could see anything but a flurry of white.

Please, God. Protect everyone who is out there searching. Protect those who are lost.

She drew a shuddery breath.

Please protect Tony. Bring him back to the lodge, safe and sound. Bring him back to...

Tears welled in her eyes.

...to me.

She closed her eyes, recalling the kiss they'd shared. Only in her imagination he didn't pull away so soon. This time his lips lingered on hers.

He remembered I preferred tea to coffee. After all these years...

She looked out at the storm again, the snow whirling and spinning past the window, resembling how she felt on the inside—confused, tossed about by a strong wind, saddened over what might have been. Tony's life was here. Hers was in California.

"Don't worry about him, Maddie."

She looked to her right where Audrey now stood.

"Tony knows this country from his boyhood and he's trekked all over it since he moved here last spring. He's no flatlander. He'll keep his wits about him."

Pride wanted Maddie to deny she was worried. Honesty wouldn't allow it. She turned her gaze out the window again. "I haven't seen snow like this in a long, long time." She shook her head. "I suppose you'd call me a flatlander."

"Mmm. Maybe. Maybe not. I've got a feeling you'd fit in around here rather nicely." She patted Maddie on the shoulder. "I'd best get back to the kitchen and give Cookie a hand."

What if Audrey was right? What if Maddie *would* fit in around there rather nicely? Was it crazy to want to?

Was it crazy to want Tony?

Tony had almost reached the top end of the logging road on Frazier Ridge when word came over the radio that the two missing skiers had been found and were okay. They were cold and hungry but uninjured. Tony said a quick prayer of thanksgiving as he turned the Sno-Cat around and headed for home.

Alone in the cab, staring at the snowy white world beyond the headlights and listening to the steady rumble of the engine, Tony allowed his thoughts to return to Maddie. This emergency had postponed their second meeting about the manuscript, but he couldn't count on anything else happening to give him more time to win her affections. Oh, he might delay a little if he pretended to consider other offers, but that would be a lie. He already knew he wanted David to have it.

Father, I can't think of anything else to do. I want her to come to know me better, to learn to care for me the way I care for her. She could be gone in a few days and then I might never see her again. So if she's the woman You have in store for me, You're going to have to do something.

Maybe Your plan is to snow her in.

He smiled at the thought. It wasn't a far-fetched idea. After all, God had been known to stop the sun in its tracks, to dry up the rains and to part the sea. Why not send a blizzard to throw two people together if that's what He wanted?

But the real question remained—was this what God wanted? Had He brought Maddie here for this purpose?

"Make it clear to both of us, Father."

Tony thought of himself as a levelheaded sort. He wasn't one to give in to sudden whims. He was more methodical in his approach to both life and business. Buying this lodge had been something he'd done with careful planning and forethought. He'd saved and re-searched and never rushed the decision.

But there was nothing levelheaded or methodical about his feelings for Maddie. The moment he saw her standing in the lobby of the lodge, he'd felt his life was about to change.

As he drew closer to town, lights from the lodge shone through the curtain of snow like a golden bea-con, welcoming him back. It made him feel good, seeing those lights and knowing everything they represented. The lodge was home to him, but it was also hope for the community. As the lodge prospered, so would other businesses in town. More skiers in the winter and more vacationers in the summer meant more dollars flow-ing into Cloud Mountain, dollars that would find their way into the schools and the fire department and the police department.

With everything in him, he wanted the lodge to succeed. He was willing to work hard and long to make it happen. And he'd been willing to do it alone. He'd been on his own all his adult life. He was used to the single life and, while he'd hoped he would one day meet the woman who was meant to be his wife, he hadn't been impatient or unhappy. He'd believed love would happen in God's good and perfect time.

Was this that time? Was Maddie the woman he'd waited for?

He hoped so…because this sure felt like love.

Chapter Twelve

Maddie didn't sleep well. Her dreams were troubled, and when she awakened, she felt as if she'd run a marathon during the night. Her muscles ached. Her ankle throbbed.

She rolled onto her side and looked at the digital clock on the nightstand. It wasn't yet six o'clock. She rolled to her other side and closed her eyes, willing herself to go back to sleep. Instead, Tony's image drifted into her mind.

After his return last night, while everyone in the lodge rejoiced over the safe return of the lost skiers, Maddie had caught him watching her, a frown pinching his forehead. Had she done something to displease him? If so, she couldn't think what.

With a sigh of exasperation, she flopped onto her back and stared upward. "Close the deal and go home. If you leave now, you'll be all right. You don't need a man in your life. You don't need to fall in love again. You just need to pay off your debts so you can stop worrying about them."

But if that's true, why does my heart hurt when I think of not seeing him again?

In the darkness of her room, she pictured Tony. She remembered him on the first day she arrived, recalled that vague sense that she should know him. She remembered how he'd carefully coached her on the bunny hill, his words of encouragement as they rode the ski lift, his concern for her when she fell. She envisioned him chopping wood and that fluttery feeling watching him had stirred in her heart. She remembered the sound of his voice lifted in worship. She recalled his infectious laughter.

Maddie grabbed a pillow and pressed it over her face as the memory of Tony's lips upon hers invaded her senses. Oh, that kiss. That wonderfully torturous sweet kiss. If only it could have gone on longer. If only he'd kissed her again and again and again.

She released a pent-up groan and tossed aside the pillow, then sat up in bed. After switching on the lamp, she reached for her robe. A few minutes later, she made her way out of her room, down the hall and through the dining room. Hopefully a cup of tea would soothe her thoughts. Of course, first she had to find where Cookie kept things in the kitchen.

The teakettle was easy. It was on the stove. She managed to take it to the sink and fill it with water while still supporting herself with her crutches. As she turned, kettle in hand, the kitchen door swung open.

Tony—clad in Levi's and a blue plaid shirt—stood in the doorway, his hair mussed from sleep, surprise widening his eyes. "Maddie?"

"I'm sorry. Did I wake you?"

"No. I'm usually the first one up. Starting the coffee brewing is my job."

She raised the kettle in her hand. "I wanted some tea."

"Here." He strode toward her. "Let me help you with that." He took the teakettle, set it on a burner and turned the knob on the stove. Looking back at her, he motioned with his head toward a stool. "Sit down and relax. It won't take long for the water to heat."

Maddie was glad to oblige. It allowed her the pleasure of watching him as he moved about the kitchen.

"Mind a little music?" he asked as he reached for a boom box and pressed the play button without waiting for an answer.

"It's beginning to look a lot like Christmas," a male voice sang through the speakers.

Tony joined in on the next line, tossing a grin in Maddie's direction, a silent invitation to sing along.

Her heart stuttered in response. She couldn't have sung a note to save her soul.

"Where will you spend Christmas, Maddie? Will you join your mom and sister in Florida?"

"Not this year."

She hadn't spent Christmas with her family in ages. When she was married, it was because Craig always had somewhere else he wanted to be. After the divorce, it was too painful to be with her sister and brother-in-law. The two were blissfully happy, as much in love today as when they'd wed fifteen years ago, and seeing them made her feel a bit sorry for herself.

She pointed at her ankle. "Good thing I didn't plan to go. I'd hate to be flying across the country with this."

Tony leaned a hip against the counter and crossed his arms over his chest. "I'm sorry about that. I shouldn't have encouraged you to go on the ski lift. We could have kept using the rope tow."

"It isn't your fault."

"It feels like it." He was silent for a short while before saying, "Why don't you stay at the lodge for Christmas?"

"Here?" Her heart skipped again.

"Why not? Doc says you shouldn't drive for a while. I'll bet David would agree that you should stay put."

Now her heart was racing. "I didn't bring enough clothes."

"That wouldn't be too hard to fix. Nobody should spend Christmas alone. Besides, you shouldn't miss the feast Cookie will prepare."

Did he ask because he wanted her to stay? Or did he feel sorry for her because she was far from family at Christmas?

The teakettle began to whistle and Tony pushed off the counter and walked to the stove. "Think about it, Maddie," he said as he poured water into a cup.

She was quite certain she would think of little else.

"You've had a silly grin on your face ever since I got here this morning." Audrey set a stack of mail on Tony's desk. "What are you so happy about?"

"Nothing in particular." His smile widened. He couldn't help it. He'd been a grinning fool ever since

he talked to Maddie that morning. The idea of her staying at the lodge over the holidays had popped into his
head suddenly and before he knew it, he'd said it aloud.
He figured that had to be a good thing. Maybe even a
God thing.

"I know you better than that, Tony. 'Fess up."

"I asked Maddie to stay for Christmas. At the lodge
with all of us."

Audrey cocked an eyebrow. "And she's going to?"

"She didn't say yes, but she didn't say no, either."

"I had a feeling about you and that young woman."

"Me, too."

Audrey turned toward the office door. "While you're
in such a good mood, you might want to think about
ordering wallpaper for some of the rooms in the east
wing. We got another reservation today and I'd hate
to have to turn anybody down because enough rooms
aren't ready."

Tony leaned back in his chair. *Thanks, Lord.* Too
many reservations was a problem he looked forward to.

He swiveled around and pulled a binder off the book-
shelf. Inside the hard blue covers were his plans and
projections for the lodge, figures and ideas that went
back several years. He opened it on his desk and flipped
through the pages.

Two hundred thousand dollars.

New roof. Remodeled kitchen. Update the heating
and air-conditioning system. What else could he do with
that amount of money? And how much higher might
Fairchild be willing to go?

Tony turned another page in the binder.

Even with all the remodeling and restoring, could the lodge provide the sort of life Maddie deserved? She was a city girl. Cloud Mountain, even with a nice lodge, would still be Cloud Mountain. Would she be happy here?

His smile was replaced with a frown.

God, have I gotten ahead of You?

He rose from the chair and walked out of his office. The lodge was quiet again. Most of the Sullivan clan were skiing or snowboarding, eager to test the fresh powder from the previous night's storm. Those who weren't on the mountain had gone into town to browse in the different tourist shops that lined Main Street.

Where was Maddie? Had she gone to town as well?

As if in answer, he heard laughter—Maddie's laughter—coming from the kitchen. He followed the irresistible sound and what he found was equally irresistible. Maddie, a smudge of flour on her cheek and another on the tip of her nose, rolling out cookie dough, her right knee resting on the seat of a chair. Cookie stood nearby, stirring something bright green in a mixing bowl.

"Ah, Tony," the chef said. "Have you come to help us?"

"Depends. What are you making?"

"Christmas cookies, of course." He held up the bowl. "Here's the frosting for the trees."

Tony crossed the kitchen and stopped on the other side of the table where Maddie was now pressing various shaped cutters into the dough. "You look like you're having a good time."

"I am." She plucked up a piece of dough and popped

it into her mouth, then closed her eyes. "Mmm. I haven't eaten cookie dough in years."

When she looked at him again, the sparkle of joy in her brown eyes took his breath away. He remembered all too well the sadness that filled them on the day she arrived.

"Here," she said, holding a spoonful of cookie dough toward him. "Indulge."

Nothing on earth could have stopped him from doing her bidding, and he didn't even *like* cookie dough.

"Good, huh?"

He swallowed the sugary gob of flour, eggs and vanilla. "Mmm. Good." Hopefully, lightning wouldn't strike him dead for telling a lie. But please don't offer me another bite.

"When I was a little girl, my mom and sister and I would spend one Saturday in December baking and frosting sugar cookies. My hands would be stained red and blue and green from the food coloring. Oh, and the little candies we sprinkled on top. I loved eating those, too. When I got older, I looked forward to the day I could revive the tradition with my own children."

And just like that, her smile was gone.

Why didn't you and Craig have kids?

Tears welled in her eyes as she answered the question he hadn't asked aloud. "Craig always said he wasn't ready to be a dad." She shrugged. "But I guess that's changed now."

He reached out and touched her cheek with his fingertips. "You deserve better, Maddie." I'd give you better.

The hint of a smile returned to her lips as she blinked

away the tears. "Thanks. I didn't mean to go all weepy on you." She waved the spoon in the air. "Must be too much sugar."

"Yeah. Must be."

She watched him in silence and Tony found himself wishing he could read her thoughts. He didn't want to frighten her off. He wanted her to feel safe with him. How could he prove that he wouldn't hurt her the way Craig had?

"Tony," Cookie said, "if you aren't going to help, leave. You're interfering with my workforce."

Maddie laughed as she handed Tony the rolling pin. "Best do as he says. You roll. I'll cut."

He was happy to oblige.

Chapter Thirteen

On Tuesday, Tony and Maddie finished their negotiations for the manuscript, agreeing to a slightly higher amount than the original offer. Everyone involved was pleased. Tony because he could speed up renovations to the lodge. Maddie because she would soon be debt-free. David because he was adding something he prized to his collection.

"The contract of sale will arrive at the lodge by Friday," David told Maddie when they talked later that day.

"Good. I'll tell Tony to expect it. I know he'll be glad when everything is signed, sealed and delivered."

"So when are you flying back to L.A.?"

She worried her lower lip.

"Maddie? Did I lose you?"

"No, I'm here. I…well, I'm not sure when I'm flying back. Tony invited me to stay at the lodge through Christmas."

"That's a great idea."

"I haven't decided yet."

"I think you should."

She stared at the red boot on her ankle, braced on the footstool in her guestroom. "You do?"

"Yes, I do. Remember the advice I gave you when you first arrived?"

"Uh-huh. Have fun, you said."

"You want to stay, don't you?"

She thought of Tony's sweet kiss two days ago. Why hadn't he tried to kiss her again? She'd wanted him to. And yesterday when she'd fed him the cookie dough, she'd thought—

"Maddie, you do want to stay, don't you?"

"Yes."

"Then stay."

"My mail must be a mile high by now."

"Nothing that can't wait a couple of weeks."

"You make me feel expendable."

"You're not expendable, Maddie, but I would like to see you happy. Really happy. I don't think you're going to find happiness through your work."

To be honest, neither did she.

"Sorry, Maddie. I've got a call on the other line I need to take. Let me know when the contracts get there."

"I will."

"Goodbye."

"'Bye."

She closed her cell phone, breaking the connection.

I think you should stay.

Maddie *could* use a vacation and it would be fun to spend Christmas with everyone at the lodge. She may not have known Tony, Audrey or Cookie for long, but she was fond of them, all the same.

Perhaps more than fond of Tony.

* * *

Standing in the center of the Uriah Small guestroom, Tony imagined different possibilities. It needed to be more than a place for guests to sleep. After all, by leaving behind that manuscript, Mr. Small was responsible for Tony's dreams for the lodge coming to fruition all the sooner.

Maybe he should turn it into a library, although he supposed that wasn't a good idea. It was too far from the center of the lodge.

He could make the room part of a suite. It could be a sitting room and the guestroom next door could be the bedroom. It would be easy enough to put a door in the connecting wall. He could buy some used editions of Uriah Small's works to fill the bookcase and, once David Fairchild had the manuscript published, they could give the new work a place of honor.

"Knock, knock."

Maddie's voice drew him around to face the door.

"Audrey told me you were up here." She swung herself into the room.

"I was going over some possibilities in my head."

"Is this the room where you found the manuscript?"

"Yeah." He pointed toward the wall. "Right over there. Sometimes I can't believe how the Lord blessed me with that find. Others could have found it long before I got here."

"What if you hadn't found it?"

He considered the question a moment before answering, "It wouldn't have changed all that much. Except how long it would take before I finished the remodeling." He smiled. "Oh, and Cookie will be happier with that new kitchen he's about to get."

She laughed softly. "He was telling me about that yesterday. He'll be in seventh heaven."

Should he ask her if she'd decided to stay for Christmas? Or should he be patient and let her tell him in her own good time? He wasn't afraid of risks in his business life. If he were, he wouldn't be the owner of this lodge. But he didn't want to risk losing Maddie.

"I talked to David a short while ago. He said he'll have the contracts delivered to you by Friday."

"Great." *Unless that means you'll be leaving.*

"Are you planning to do something special with this room?" She used her crutches to draw closer to Tony.

"That's what I was thinking. Something special. But I'm not sure what."

"This would make a lovely sitting room for a suite." She moved to one of the windows. "You can see the town from here and the mountain from over there."

He wanted to hold her and kiss her, if for no other reason than she'd matched his own idea for the room. Except there *were* other reasons. Lots of them. He was hungry to take her in his arms, to tell her he loved her, to ask her to stay so that they could talk about every change made to the lodge, so he could hear her ideas, so they could plan things together.

She looked at him again.

A man could drown in her eyes.

"Tony, I'd like to accept your invitation to stay at the lodge through Christmas."

He stepped toward her. Say something. Tell her you're glad she's going to stay.

"It will be a nice change from L.A. I haven't seen a white Christmas in ten years at least."

"I guarantee it'll be white." He reached out and cupped the side of her face with his hand.

She leaned into his touch, a movement so slight he wasn't sure it happened.

He spoke her name on a breath.

She smiled.

Ker-thump went his heart. He was growing used to it by now.

From the end of the hall, Audrey's voice intruded on the moment. "Tony, you're needed on the telephone."

"Can you take a message?" he called back, not wanting to move, not wanting to think, not wanting to breathe.

"He says it's important."

Maddie drew back. "You'd better take it."

"Wait here. I won't be long. We can talk over a few more ideas for this room."

She nodded, her smile tenuous.

Tony turned on his heel and strode from the room. Whoever was on the phone would be sorry if what they had to say wasn't important.

He took the stairs two at a time, entered his office and yanked the phone from its cradle. "Tony Anderson speaking."

"Mr. Anderson," the voice on the other end of the line said, "my name is Phillip Endicott. I represent Mariah Kent. Ms. Kent is the great-niece of Uriah Small and the legal heir to his estate."

With those last few words, Tony felt the bottom drop out of his world.

"Ms. Kent recently learned that you've discovered some of her uncle's last remaining work."

"Yes."

"I'm sure you'll understand that she is eager to have the property returned to her."

Returned to her.

No contract to sign with David Fairchild.

No discussions about how to turn the room upstairs into the Uriah Small suite.

No money to speed things along.

No new roof.

No new kitchen.

Just like that, back to square one.

Tony said something about having his attorney contact Mr. Endicott, asked for a little more information and hung up the phone.

God, what are You doing?

He sank onto his desk chair. Five years. His original plan had called for it to take at least five years to finish the work on the lodge and begin to turn a profit. And there might not ever be a large profit. Enough but not a lot. Enough for him but maybe not enough for a wife and family.

Maddie deserves better than I have to offer.

With a heavy heart, he picked up the telephone and dialed the number for his attorney.

Chapter Fourteen

The mood around the lodge was subdued in the days following that fateful phone call. Even the Sullivans were affected by the news.

"Maybe you can fight this," Sam Sullivan told Tony. "If there's anything I can do, I'd be glad to help. It just seems wrong that this woman can take the manuscript after you found it."

"If she's the rightful heir, she should have it." It pained Tony to say those words, but he knew they were true. "All I can do now is wait and see what my attorney advises. But thanks for the offer. I appreciate it."

Sam wasn't the only person offering help, advice and sympathy. As word spread, the citizens of Cloud Mountain showed up at the lodge. Pastor Luke came to pray with Tony. Evie Barrett brought sweets from the candy store. Gary Patterson and his sister, Betina, offered to lend a hand with wallpaper hanging or painting or whatever else he might need. And there were others who came, many others, all of them asking what they could do.

Tony appreciated the expressions of kindness more than he could say, but while the loss of the manuscript—and what that could have meant for the lodge—was a great disappointment, it was knowing he had nothing much to offer Maddie that broke his heart. How could he ask her to choose Cloud Mountain over L.A., to choose managing a struggling lodge over closing deals for David Fairchild? It wouldn't be fair to her.

Maddie observed the show of concern from Tony's friends and wished she could be one of them. But something happened on the day he took that phone call. He'd erected an invisible wall between them and Maddie didn't know how to tear it down.

"I don't know, David." Lying on her back on the bed, she stared at the ceiling of her guestroom. "Maybe I should come home for Christmas after all. I could hire someone to drive me to Boise so I could turn in the rental car and catch a flight to L.A. There doesn't seem to be much reason to stay now."

"What do you mean, Maddie?"

"Well, with the rightful ownership of the manuscript up in the air, we can't close the deal and—"

"Wait. You weren't going to stay because of business. You were going to stay because Tony asked you to. You were going to make a holiday of it."

Her chest felt as if it were being squeezed by an iron band.

David's voice hardened. "He didn't take back the invitation, did he?"

"No, but—"

"Then why leave?"

Tears slipped from her eyes, leaving damp tracks along her temples and into her hair. "Because I don't think he wants me here. I'm a reminder of what he almost had but lost, of all the things he won't be able to do with the lodge for now."

"If that's true, he isn't the man I thought he was. But I'm betting it isn't true. Don't run away, Maddie."

How could she tell David that she was afraid to stay? She knew too well what it was like to love someone who didn't love her in return. She never wanted to experience that pain again.

Only, deep down, she knew it was too late to escape the pain. She'd already fallen in love with Tony Anderson. With Tony and this lodge and Audrey and Cookie. With the quaint little town and the people who lived in it. With Redeemer Community Church and the Candy Corner and the medical clinic. Even with that miserable spot on the mountain where she'd broken her ankle.

"Think about it, Maddie, and call me again tomorrow."

"Okay," she whispered, her throat too tight for much sound.

As soon as she closed the phone, she rolled onto her side and curled into a ball, praying the ache in her heart would stop soon.

Tony drove the Sno-Cat along the same road he and his guests had taken in Nick Robertson's sleigh the previous week. Only now the sun shone in a clear sky overhead and the light reflected off the snow as if from a million diamonds. At the lookout point at the top of the hill, he pulled into the parking lot and cut the engine. Silence enveloped the cab.

He stared down at the picture-postcard view of Cloud Mountain, remembering how long he'd planned for the day that he could move here to live. He'd wanted it. He'd worked for it.

Now there was something—some*one*—he wanted even more. What was he going to do about Maddie?

In the stillness of the snowy hilltop, he thought of Jacob and Rebekah from the Bible. Jacob had loved Rebekah so much he worked for seven years to gain her hand in marriage and, after being tricked by her father, he worked another seven.

What are you ready to do to win Maddie's love?

Would he work for seven years?

Yes.

Would he give up the lodge and Cloud Mountain?

He held his breath, unsure what his heart would answer.

Yes, I would.

It surprised him, the certainty he felt, but it was true. If he had to, he would follow Maddie to California. He would return to the corporate treadmill. If that's what it took, he was willing.

He loved her that much.

He started the Sno-Cat's engine and turned the vehicle toward town.

Audrey stepped from behind the desk in the lobby. "I'm not sure where Tony went, but he took the Sno-

Cat. He may be out for a while. Is there something I can do for you?"

"No." Maddie took a deep breath and released it. "I've been thinking I'd ask one of the Sullivans to drive me to Boise in my rental car on Sunday since they'll be going that way themselves."

"But Tony said you were staying for Christmas."

"I was, but…" She shrugged. "I'm not certain I should now."

"Well, *I'm* certain," the woman replied, emphasizing her words with an abrupt nod of her head.

Maddie gave her a tremulous smile. "Thanks, Audrey."

She turned away, not wanting to risk the return of her tears. It already felt as if she were saying goodbye to too much. She decided to go to her room to begin packing. Even though she would be here a couple more days, it didn't hurt to get an early start.

She had almost arrived at her room when the back door opened and Tony stepped into view. Maddie's heart tripped at the sight of him.

If only…

"Maddie, would you take a ride with me in the Sno-Cat?"

She should say no. Being near him was too hard. "Okay."

"Great." He smiled, and her heart tripped again. "Where's your coat?"

"In here." She slid the key card into the reader and opened the door to her room. "I'll get it."

"I'll wait."

She didn't know what this was about. She didn't care, not if it was responsible for making him smile again.

A short while later, Tony carried her out to the Sno-Cat and deposited her on the passenger seat of the cab before running around to the driver's side and hopping in.

"Where are we going?"

He started the engine. "Just up the hill a ways. It won't take us long to get there."

More questions swirled in her mind, but she didn't ask them. She decided to enjoy the interlude. It would be over all too soon. Reality would come crashing in and by Sunday she would say goodbye to Tony.

But not yet. It wasn't here yet.

She patted the side panel of the door. "This is really something. I've never been in a Sno-Cat before."

"Not much use for them in L.A."

"No." She looked out the window. Here was one more thing she would miss. "I suppose not."

"I got a good deal on this one. It's come in handy more than once this winter."

I don't want to talk about the Sno-Cat. I want to tell you I've lost my heart to you. I want to ask you to kiss me again and to hold me close and never let me go.

"Look." Tony pointed toward the edge of the forest. "A fox."

Maddie followed the direction of his hand but all she saw was a flash of reddish brown as it disappeared into the trees.

"In the summer, we get lots of deer and elk in these parts. When I was a kid, my aunt and uncle had trouble with a bear who thought their garbage can was his personal smorgasbord. Man, my aunt would get so angry when she had to clean up the mess that bear left behind."

"Where was their cabin?"

"Back the other side of town about two and a half miles."

The Sno-Cat climbed a hillside, rumbling and grumbling along. Maddie thought this must be a lot like riding in a tank, except without suffering from claustrophobia—the Cat had plenty of windows. At the top of the hill, Tony turned the vehicle into a parking area and came to a halt a few feet before reaching the guardrail. Then he turned off the engine.

The silence was so complete it startled Maddie. She held her breath, not wanting to disturb it.

"I came up here to think a while ago," Tony said. "I was thinking about all the stuff I couldn't do without that manuscript to sell."

"I'm so sorry."

"No. Listen, Maddie. I have something I need to say." He pointed again. "Look down there. See the town? That's the kind of place I want to live. The people who have been coming by the lodge all week? They're the kind of people I want for my friends and neighbors."

She nodded, understanding why he felt that way. She felt it, too, and she'd been here only a short while.

"But, Maddie?"

Something about his tone—soft, gentle, almost like a caress—caused her to look at him.

"There's something I want far more than the lodge or this town or my friends and neighbors."

Blood began to pound in her ears. "There is?"

"You, Maddie. I want you." He cupped her chin with his hand. "I love you. Some might think it happened too fast. Maybe you think it's too fast. But my feelings are real."

Tears caused his image to swim before her eyes.

"I know you've got debts to pay and I know the lodge won't make us lots of money. It'll take time before it's able to turn much of a profit. I think we could manage, but success won't happen overnight. But if you need to go back to California, then I'm willing to come there. I'm willing to do whatever it takes for us to be together. Just let me know if I've got a ghost of a chance to win your love."

Something happened in that moment. It was as if fear had been cut from her heart, leaving room for trust to move in. Maybe God had been working that miracle from the start of her trip to Idaho, but it was completed in the cab of this Sno-Cat on a hillside overlooking Cloud Mountain.

Awed by the wonder of it all, she shook her head from side to side as the tears fell from her eyes, streaking her cheeks.

"Not even a chance, Maddie?"

She blinked back more tears. "No, that isn't what I meant. Tony, I couldn't ask you to leave Cloud Mountain." She drew a quick breath. "I don't want to leave, either. Not ever. And I...I don't want to leave you."

Tony's hands cradled her face as they drew closer to each other. Their lips met and she tasted the salt of her tears. The kiss ended, but they didn't draw back. They remained close, their foreheads almost touching.

"Maddie, I pledge to you my faithfulness. As God is my witness, I'll never be untrue to you."

She believed him. With nothing held back, she believed in his love and his faithfulness and his steadfastness. She didn't need him or anyone to tell her that he spoke the truth. She believed him to the very center of her heart, a place once abandoned but now filled to overflowing with joy.

December was once again her favorite month.

Epilogue

Christmas Morning, one year later

Maddie glanced at the clock on the nightstand. It was only 4:30 a.m., but she was wide-awake. Upstairs in the east wing, her mom slept in one of the guestrooms, while a few doors down the hall from her, in the Uriah Small suite, David and Lois did the same. Before breakfast, they would all gather in the reading room to open Christmas gifts, but that was still a few hours away.

However, it wasn't the anticipation of opening presents that made her sleepless. It was something far better.

"Merry Christmas," Tony whispered, his voice low and gravelly. "Can't sleep?"

She couldn't see her husband in the darkness of the bedroom, but she didn't need to see him to know that he slept on his back, one arm flung over his head. Not after six months as his wife.

She turned onto her side and laid her head on his shoulder. "No, I can't sleep."

"Were you like this as a kid? Can I expect this every Christmas morning?"

"Yes. I'm always the first one awake."

"Hmm. I've always been the one who slept in."

"That'll never do." She laughed softly. "Besides, I'm surprised you could sleep at all after David's big news. Can you believe he's put together that group to invest in the resort in such a short amount of time? Another lift. A snowmaking machine. Some condos. I knew he liked it here in Cloud Mountain, but I didn't know how much."

"Yeah." There was a smile in his voice now. "I'll bet the news has already traveled from one end of town to the other. This is going to mean lots of new jobs."

"You know…" she lifted her head to kiss him on the cheek "…maybe we'll have so many guests staying at the lodge that we'll have to think about moving into a house of our own."

"That would be great. Maybe next year or the one after. Things won't change overnight."

She drew in a deep breath and let it out. "I was thinking…it might be a good idea to look for a house before… before the baby comes."

"Before the—" Tony sat up and switched on the bedside lamp.

Her head now on the pillow, she squinted at him in the sudden glare of light. "Merry Christmas, Daddy."

"We're having a baby?" He drew her up and into his arms. "We're having a baby?"

"Uh-huh."

"When?"

"August."

Tony kissed her then, with all the sweetness, all the tenderness she had come to expect from his kisses.

Who could have thought her life would be so different today than it was when she arrived at this lodge one year ago, her heart wounded and unable to trust? Wishing for love but not daring to dream.

God thought it. That's who.

She smiled as she nestled into Tony's embrace and pondered the miracle of love.

Thank You, Jesus. And happy birthday.

* * * * *

Questions For Discussion

1. Trust is an issue for Maddie. How does her level of trust in those around her build throughout the story? How does prayer help her? How has it helped you in similar situations?

2. Tony worked steadily for years, trusting that doing so would help him achieve his dream. What parallels do you see here to the story of Jacob? How did God deliver more than Tony had expected? How has this happened in your life?

3. During the difficult years of her marriage, Maddie had to find and create a supportive circle outside her marriage. What role did David and his wife fill for her? What role did her church fill? Where do you see the members of the Cloud Mountain community fitting in?

4. In the wake of his parents' death, Tony also acquired a supportive group of friends. How does his compare to Maddie's? Does the Sullivan family seem to need a similar group of friends? Why or why not? Who in your life provides the emotional support you need?

5. Ultimately, Maddie realized she needed to reprioritize work, faith and personal relationships in her life and create a new way of approaching life day to day. How do you think this will help her going forward? What difficulties do you see for her in the future? How will her relationship with Tony help or hinder her prioritizing?

A MATCH MADE
FOR CHRISTMAS

Kathryn Springer

To Robin B.
Who provides a cozy chair, a cup of tea
and encouraging words when
I need them the most.

Chapter One

When he had to brake for a herd of whitetail deer bounding across the road, Connor Lawe knew he was home. He just hadn't expected it to feel so good. He'd shaken the hometown dust from his heels at eighteen and hadn't looked back. Not that there'd been much to look back *at*. At least from his perspective.

The changes he saw as he drove into Jackson Lake, Wisconsin were good ones, no doubt orchestrated by the small group of his classmates who'd stayed and gotten themselves elected to key positions on the city council and school board. *Good for them.* He hadn't been content to let his future be restricted by the city limits of his hometown. And even if he'd been tempted to stay, his father would have had his bags packed and waiting before the punch at his graduation party hit room temperature.

Connor navigated his way through a subdivision that had replaced a stand of pines where he and some friends had once built a fort, then passed a large snow-covered sign serving as a marker for a new sports field. When he was a kid, he'd played baseball in a dirt lot next to Roscoe's Diner.

Don't go getting all sentimental now. You know the saying. You can't go home again.

But there were exceptions to every rule.

A grown son—and an only child—had to come home again if his dad needed him. And it didn't matter whether or not Robert Lawe *admitted* he needed him. Which was why Connor was fresh off an early morning flight at an airport with—count them—two runways, driving the only rental available, a twenty-year-old dinosaur that ground the gears as if there were a sausage factory operating under the hood.

Connor took a left turn onto Jackson Avenue, which wound a casual path through the heart of the city. The locals affectionately referred to it as The Avenue. Winter had stripped the leaves from the sugar maples lining the street, creating a living picket fence. Snow-dusted wreaths lashed to the antique street lamps reminded Connor that the upcoming holiday had given him the perfect excuse for a visit. According to the music pumping through the crackling speakers of the car radio, *everyone* came home for Christmas.

Like his dad was going to fall for that. Christmas hadn't brought Connor back to Jackson Lake in twelve years, but at the moment, it was the only excuse he had and he was going to use it.

The Avenue took a gentle curve to the right and Connor's foot tapped the brake. He knew what was ahead, but the sight of the three-story brick building still squeezed his heart with an emotion he wasn't in the mood to analyze. *The Jackson Lake News*. Cornerstone of the downtown. Built at the turn of the century by the city founders—a group of rough lumberjacks with a vision for the future. His great-grandfather had been one of them.

Connor parked the car along the curb and stepped out. Snow poured over the tops of his shoes, but the avalanche over his favorite loafers didn't compare to the avalanche of memories that crashed over him when he walked into the building.

"Can I help you?" The gray-haired receptionist sitting at a desk behind the counter glanced up at him and then did a double take. "Connor!"

Cecily Verne had been like an adoptive mother to him while he was growing up. She'd even made him a pirate costume for the fifth grade play. Connor stretched across the counter and she met him halfway. He wrapped an arm around her and felt her shoulders shake. "Hey, Cissy."

"No one's called me that for…" Her eyes were moist when she stepped back and studied him. "Ten years?"

"Twelve." But who was counting? "Is he here?"

"Where else would he be?" Cecily's eyes flashed with disapproval and she waved toward the swinging doors separating the front office from the newsroom. "He's in a meeting with the reporters, so I guess you made it just in time."

Connor didn't respond to the question in her voice. Not yet, anyway. He winked at her. "I'll take a seat in the back."

Robert was expecting him but not until the weekend.

All it had taken was one long-distance conversation with Walter Parish, his dad's cardiologist, and Connor had called in a few more overdue vacation days. Dr. Parish, who happened to be one of Robert's golfing buddies, hadn't broken confidentiality but he *had* dropped a strong hint that Connor should stop traipsing around the world and convince Robert to slow down.

Connor figured that could only be done in person. With some duct tape and really thick rope.

He wound his way through the maze of cubicles to the conference room. The solid oak door couldn't completely muffle his father's familiar bellow on the other side. Connor eased the door open and slipped inside.

"It's that time of year again, people. We've got a Christmas issue to put together in less than a month."

Connor smiled as a low groan took a lap around the table. "I don't like it any more than you do, but the readers expect it. That means everyone has to go out and find a warm, fuzzy Christmas story. Something guaranteed to bring a tear to Scrooge's eye."

Connor's eyes met his dad's across the table.

"And I mean *everyone.*"

This time Connor stifled a groan.

Welcome home.

Sarah Kendle had a mutiny on her hands. Fortunately, the seventh grade girls threatening to revolt were relatively harmless. Most days.

"We bake cookies for the Christmas Eve service *every* year. Can't we do something different?" Jennifer Sands, the group's unofficial spokeswoman, flopped down in one of the bowl-shaped chairs that were scattered throughout the youth room. A chorus of agreement rose from her loyal entourage.

"What do you have in mind?" Sarah asked, keeping her voice mild.

The girls exchanged looks. Just as Sarah suspected, they didn't know what they *wanted* to do—they only knew what they didn't.

"We don't know. Just *not* cookies!"

Sarah knew from experience the few moments of silence that followed wouldn't last long. Except this time it was Emma White who raised a tentative hand to get her attention.

"You said that everyone gets so busy this time of year, they forget the real meaning of Christmas. Why don't we do something to help people remember?"

The other girls stared at Emma in astonishment. Painfully shy, Emma pitched in whenever she was asked to help but rarely expressed her opinion. Until now. Maybe that's why the rest of the girls looked eager to embrace it.

Sarah offered up a silent prayer of thanks. The last two times she and the girls had met, lengthy wish lists and sharing plans for their Christmas vacations had dominated the conversation. Sarah had gone home both nights feeling discouraged. She wanted to make a difference in their lives. Wanted their faith to take root during these years so they could stand strong as adults. There'd been times over the past four months she'd wondered why she'd thought she could lead a tiny band of middle school girls, but now she felt a stirring of hope.

"Okay. That's a great idea, Emma. Does anyone have any ideas how we could do that?"

For the next half hour, ideas flew back and forth while Sarah took notes on the dry erase board. She kept an eye on Emma, who'd lapsed into silence after starting the discussion. The girl sat cross-legged on the floor, her Bible in her lap, oblivious to the laughter bouncing around the room.

"What are you reading, Emma?"

The room suddenly went quiet, as if Alyssa Courtman had shouted the question instead of whispering it. Twin circles of color dotted Emma's cheeks.

Everyone waited patiently until Emma gathered the courage to speak. "But the angel said to them, 'Do not be afraid. I bring you good news of great joy that will be for all the people. Today in the town of David a Savior has been born to you; He is Christ, the Lord.'"

"What are you reading *that* for?" Mandi Peters frowned.

Sarah felt a familiar stab of frustration. Mandi only came to church on Wednesday evenings because her mother forced her to. The preteen had made that announcement the first time they'd met. Mandi wasn't a disruption—she was too busy penning intricate designs on the knees of her jeans or staring at the clock—but Sarah had been fervently praying she would find a way to break through some of the walls Mandi had in place.

"That's what we want people to remember," Emma said simply, not intimidated by Mandi's scowl. "The good news."

"We could take out an ad in the newspaper," Jennifer suggested.

Sarah winced. Robert Lawe, the editor of *The Jackson Lake News*, published a special Christmas issue once a year because his readers expected it, but she'd heard him speak at several chamber of commerce meetings since she'd moved to Jackson Lake, where he'd unapologetically described himself as a "self-made man." Apparently God hadn't had anything to do with his success. She could only imagine his response to a full-page ad proclaiming the Christmas story.

"That wouldn't work." Mandi crossed her arms. "People wouldn't read it."

Jennifer, used to having immediate agreement to every idea she came up with, pouted for a second. "So what do *you* think we should do?"

Mandi stiffened but Alyssa, always the peacemaker, dove into the conversation. "We could say it in person."

Jennifer's eyebrow lifted. "You mean just walk up to someone and tell them God loves them?"

Alyssa held her ground. "Why not?"

"Like a singing telegram?" Mandi snickered. "Only without the singing and the clown suit?"

Alyssa looked offended but suddenly Emma giggled. Which started a chain reaction. Within sixty seconds, all the girls were doubled over.

An idea was beginning to form in Sarah's mind. A *crazy* idea. Or maybe not…

"No clown suits." Sarah waited until the giggling subsided a bit. "But let's not rule out the singing part yet."

Chapter Two

Roscoe's Diner was as much a city landmark as *The Jackson Lake News*. Connor sat alone in a lumpy vinyl booth by the window, taking comfort in the knowledge that the onion rings were still deep-fried in grease, the coffee was strong enough to dissolve the end of a spoon and Roscoe himself was stomping around the kitchen like a cantankerous grizzly. He rarely left his lair but when he saw Connor's name scrawled at the top of his order, he poked his head out.

"Heard a rumor you were coming back," he snorted. "Surprised you're here instead of at that fancy bookstore down the street, sipping one of those nonfat decaf latte things that smell like bubble bath."

"You always had a way with words, Roscoe. You should have been a reporter." Connor couldn't help but grin. Twelve years hadn't changed Roscoe a bit. Unkempt salt-and-pepper hair sprang in every direction like an unclipped hedge. A grimy canvas apron stretched across his barrel-shaped torso. The faded tattoos covering his arms told stories of a war that Connor had only read about in history books.

"Got better things to do with my time than decorate the stuff people use to line their birdcages," Roscoe growled.

Connor laughed, saluting him with the bent spoon he'd used to stir his coffee. "Fair enough."

Roscoe grunted again and disappeared. Bev, the waitress whose frizzy red hair clashed with her lavender eyeshadow, sauntered over to his table with the coffeepot. She rolled her eyes at the kitchen. "Don't mind him. He's been in a bad mood since the day he was born."

She refilled his cup then targeted the table packed with students from the community college who'd commandeered the back corner of the diner and turned it into a study area. They took up space at Roscoe's because the hamburgers were cheap and the water—straight from the kitchen tap—was free.

Connor stared at the blank screen on his laptop. The cursor blinked in the corner, waiting for him to write something profound. No. Not profound. That wasn't what Robert wanted from him. If Connor hadn't been so ticked off at his dad, he might have appreciated his strategy. Robert couldn't have picked a better way to prove to the rest of the staff that he wasn't going to play favorites. When Connor had offered to help out at the newspaper for a few weeks, this wasn't exactly what he'd had in mind.

The door swung open, letting in a gust of wind and high-pitched laughter that shattered the peace and quiet of the diner. Connor got ready to level a look as icy as the temperature outside at whoever happened to make eye contact with him first, but the girls who stumbled in didn't even glance his way.

He blinked, just to make sure what he was seeing wasn't a figment of his imagination. No. They were still there. A giggling group of *angels*? They'd shed their winter jackets, revealing long white robes and slightly crumpled wings. Ropes of garland encircled their heads and their boots were spray-painted metallic gold.

Bev emerged from the kitchen and the coffeepot wobbled in her hand. Connor winced, preparing for the crash.

"What in the world—" She mouthed the words.

The door opened again and a young woman dashed in, carrying a trumpet. *A trumpet.* Connor had a sudden urge to smile. She wasn't in costume but she was clearly in charge of the raggedy band because the girls stopped giggling and looked to her for direction. She was in her mid-to-late twenties and there was nothing remotely angelic about *her*. The rust-colored old corduroy peacoat matched the reddish brown curls escaping from her knitted cap. A long denim skirt brushed the tops of ankle-high suede boots. Boots that were snow-covered but not painted gold.

"Can I...help you?" Bev glanced nervously toward the kitchen, where Roscoe's stream of complaints rose above the hiss of the grill.

"We're delivering a Good News-gram," one of the girls announced cheerfully. Her bright red hair matched her enthusiasm. "To Mr. Roscoe."

"Mr., um, Roscoe?" Bev carefully set the coffee-pot down on the counter and groped for something to hold on to.

"Bev! Got a order up." The roar from the kitchen made everyone flinch. Connor settled himself more comfortably in the booth. This was getting interesting. The young woman in charge took a tentative step forward as the angels crowded together like a herd of sheep who sensed a wolf in their midst.

"Roscoe, you've got some…visitors." Bev nearly choked on the word.

"Visitors?" The word rumbled out long and loud like a freight train crossing a bumpy track. "I don't want visitors unless they're *customers*."

"It's all right, girls." The young woman gathered her troop in close as footsteps thudded against worn linoleum. Roscoe emerged from the kitchen, shaking his head like an angry bull.

One of the girls squeaked.

The whole diner watched in fascination.

The redheaded girl smiled bravely at him. "Mr. Roscoe?"

Roscoe's eyes bulged when he saw them. "I ain't buying no cookies this year so you can all just fly right back out that door—"

An off-key trumpet blast drowned him out. Roscoe's mouth dropped open.

Another angel stepped forward and blew a strand of tinsel out of her eyes. Short and round, with serious blue eyes and a sweet expression, she reminded Connor of a china doll. "Mr. Roscoe? We're here to deliver a Good News-gram from your sister, Maureen."

Roscoe's jaw began to work and everyone braced themselves for the eruption. Instead, he scratched the stubble on his chin. "Maureen sent you?" His voice didn't come out at a roar this time. It was low and slightly confused.

The young woman gave the girls an encouraging look and they formed a semicircle. A thin dark-haired girl flitted around, straightening everyone's wings before taking her place with the rest of the group again.

"Behold!" The carrot-top lifted up her arms and the sleeves of her robe wrinkled like an accordion. "We bring you good news of great joy. God sent His son to Earth because He loves you. And your sister does, too."

There was a crackling sound and then, out of nowhere, music began to play. Everyone in the diner strained to hear it. Connor vaguely recognized the tune. The girls waited a few beats and then started to sing the words. They started out soft but grew more confident, spiraling into the final chorus with clear, rippling sopranos. "O Come All Ye Faithful." That was it. He remembered singing the Christmas carol when his mother took him to the Christmas Eve service—the only time they went to church as a family.

When they finished, Roscoe stepped closer, practically nose to nose with the girls. Connor drew in a breath, hoping the grouchy old cook wouldn't be too hard on them. After all, it was clear they'd been hired to deliver...what had they called it? A Good News-gram?

He watched in disbelief as Roscoe lifted the corner of his apron and dabbed at his eye.

"Onions," he muttered. "*Bev!* Get these rug rats some hot chocolate. On the house."

"Thanks, Mr. Roscoe!" The girls surrounded him and Roscoe's cheeks turned red. Finally, he shook them loose and charged back to the kitchen. Where, Connor guessed, life would make sense again.

The young woman tucked the trumpet under her arm and shepherded the girls toward one of the larger booths in the back of the diner.

They skipped right past Connor's table. When the woman brushed close enough for him to breathe in the appealing combination of fresh air and the subtle floral scent that clung to her jacket, he turned and planted one foot in the aisle.

"That was quite a show. Are you going to pass a hat?" he murmured.

She paused and looked down at him, tilting her head as if she hadn't heard him right. With the quick eye for detail his career had fine-tuned, he catalogued her features. Mouth a shade too wide. Chin a little sharp— what some people might call "heart-shaped." And her eyes…a vibrant aquamarine.

"We don't charge money to deliver Good News-grams," she said quietly. "We don't even accept donations."

"Just hot chocolate."

The aquamarine eyes widened in surprise and she took a half step forward. And bumped into his foot.

Connor wasn't quite ready for her to leave. "So what's the point?"

"To remind people why we celebrate Christmas. And to deliver a personal message from someone who loves them. Don't you think this is the perfect time of year to remind a person they're loved?"

She stepped over his foot. It must have been a hypothetical question because she didn't give him time to formulate an answer. Not that Miss Do Good would have wanted to hear it. Connor brooded over her response for a few minutes. There had to be more to it than what she claimed. His eyes drifted to the blinking cursor on the laptop again and a slow smile spread across his face.

He'd just found *his* warm, fuzzy Christmas story.

"That man is staring at us again," Alyssa whispered.

Sarah didn't have to be told. She could *feel* the weight of the stranger's gaze. For some reason, it unnerved her more than the sight of Roscoe bearing down on them like a cranky badger. She'd been more than ready to explain what the Good News-grams were all about after he'd stopped her—until she saw the gleam in his silver-gray eyes. He was a skeptic. The girls had done a good thing and then some mocking twenty-first-century *Scrooge* challenged their motives.

Scrooge wasn't exactly accurate, though, Sarah admitted to herself, resisting the urge to sneak another look at him. The man in the booth was a lot younger than the Dicken's character. And a lot more attractive.

She shook that pesky thought aside. In her opinion, character counted more than looks.

"I've seen him before," Emma murmured, licking the back of her spoon and leaving a chocolate mustache on her upper lip.

"You have?" Sarah refused to turn around and gawk at him, even though he didn't seem to have a problem gawking at them.

"Maybe your dad arrested him once." Mandi's eyes gleamed.

Oh, great.

The girls' parents, especially Emma's father, a sergeant with the local police department, had expressed their doubts about letting their daughters traipse around town dressed like angels. Sarah had assured them she'd keep a close eye on the girls but if Pastor Phillips hadn't stepped in to support their unconventional idea, she doubted the parents would've granted their permission.

The announcement about the Good News-grams had been made during the morning worship service on Sunday and right afterward Sarah had been approached by an elderly woman who wanted a message delivered to her brother. The girls had been ecstatic. And so was Sarah. Until she found out their very first message was to be delivered to Roscoe.

Roscoe's Diner was located on the south side of Jackson Avenue. It wasn't that the neighborhood was unsafe, just a bit more…colorful. Its character hadn't been created by the group of city planners who'd worked to renovate the downtown area over the past five years. If the rumors Sarah had heard were true, Roscoe had formed his own group to *counteract* the renovation. Six months of negotiation ended when the south side business owners stubbornly refused to change their storefronts to match the other businesses. The result was a two-block section at the end of The Avenue that reminded Sarah of eccentric cousins at a family reunion. The rest of the family knew they were there but did their best to ignore them.

"Girls, it's getting late. I better get you home before your parents start to worry." She left a tip for the waitress, who'd filled up the girls' cups *twice* and added extra marshmallows to their hot chocolate. "Coats on. Careful with your wings."

"When is our next delivery?" Jennifer asked, carefully tucking her red hair under her hat.

"As soon as we—"

The man in the booth suddenly loomed in front of her. "Did I hear you mention you're doing this again? Is this some kind of club?"

"Just until Christmas," Jennifer spoke up. "Our church is sponsoring us—"

Sarah ignored him and ushered the girls toward the door. He followed them with the focus of a hound dog on a rabbit trail. "What church is that?"

There was that cynical undercurrent in his voice again. Sarah's teeth ground together. Sure. Now he probably thought they were part of some religious scam.

"Lakeshore Community Fellowship. Your port in life's storms," Jennifer sang out cheerfully, always willing to add a stray sheep to the flock. The girl was a natural evangelist.

Sarah gave Jennifer a gentle nudge forward but apparently the man's curiosity still wasn't satisfied. He stepped in front of her. Sarah didn't consider herself petite but she had to tilt her head back to look at him. A half smile slashed one corner of his mouth and he handed her a business card.

"I'd appreciate it if you would call this number in the morning."

The girls, clustered in the doorway, giggled. Sarah felt her cheeks heat up. Just to get rid of him, she stuffed the card in her coat pocket and shooed the girls out of the diner as quickly as possible.

She forgot about him until her fingers closed around the card while she searched for her apartment key an hour later. Gorgeous or not, there was no way she was calling this guy. With a flick of her wrist she sent the card flying toward the wastebasket. It missed the mark and landed in Keebler's water dish.

Sighing, Sarah retrieved the soggy piece of paper before Keebler got thirsty. Her cat wasn't the most easygoing creature. Sarah's curiosity got the best of her and she glanced at the card.

Connor Lawe.

She knew the name. Robert Lawe's son. She'd heard all about him at the chamber of commerce meetings. Jackson Lake's very own hometown hero. Award-winning journalist.

This time, she didn't miss the wastebasket. Her high school gym teacher would've been proud.

Chapter Three

"Don't think I don't know what you're up to."

Connor glanced up from the front page of last week's edition of the newspaper and found himself caught in the crosshairs of his father's legendary scowl. Knowing he'd fail miserably at appearing wide-eyed and innocent, he tried confused instead. "Up to?"

Robert snorted—proving that even though his heart might be weakening, there was nothing wrong with his head. "So much for doctor-patient confidentiality," he muttered. "I ought to have Walter's license for this."

"I came home for Christmas, Dad. You know. Twinkling lights. The smell of a fresh-cut balsam. Family togetherness. Christmas carols sung by the fire…"

Robert rolled his eyes. "You disappoint me, son. I can't believe you think I'd fall for that one. Especially considering you chose to stay away all these years."

"*Chose* to stay away?" Someone had a faulty memory and it wasn't him. "Ah…Dad, you kicked me out after graduation. I believe your exact words were, 'Don't come back until you make something of yourself.'"

"How did I know it was going to take you so long?" Robert complained.

Connor's concern overrode his urge to laugh. After silently observing his dad at the newspaper the day before, he assumed Dr. Parish had exaggerated Robert's condition. Until he got home from Roscoe's and caught his father leaning against the wall, one hand pressed protectively against his chest. As soon as Robert realized he'd been spotted, he'd straightened and pretended to search for something in his shirt pocket.

Robert was a master at hiding his feelings. Connor shook his head at the irony. A career in journalism wasn't the only thing passed down from father to son.

"I'm here now—and thanks for putting me to work." Connor kept his voice casual, wondering if his dad was going to see through that, too. "Not that I'm thrilled with your choice of assignments."

Liar.

On cue, his memory conjured up an image of lively blue-green eyes and full lips curved into a smile. Well, they had been smiling. Until he'd insulted her. He had a knack for rubbing people the wrong way. Some people could play an instrument or paint portraits, he ticked people off. Connor viewed it as a necessary skill for his career. When people got emotional, their brains had a tendency to shut down and their mouths took over. But he hadn't had that effect on the woman in the diner. She'd gone all quiet and dignified on him, her eyes flashing just once in reproof before she walked away. For some reason, he'd felt a stab of something that might qualify as *guilt*. Definitely not a feeling he was used to.

"I've got reporters who'd go on strike if I made them cover the Christmas bazaar at the hospital and sent you to city hall for a real story." A glint of humor flickered in Robert's eyes. "I hope you can live it down."

"I'll survive." Although Connor knew any story he wrote that didn't draw blood would end up in his mailbox with personal critiques from his colleagues scrawled in the margins. He drained the contents of his cup and rose to his feet. "Come on. I'll drive you to work."

"Not in that contraption you came home in, I hope."

"No?" Connor's eyebrow lifted. "I thought you liked living dangerously."

Robert's lips twitched. In their verbal fencing match, Connor had just scored a point.

By noon, Connor had a makeshift office in a windowless cubicle and a Reuben sandwich with extra kraut. But no phone messages. He'd seen the wary look in the woman's eyes when he'd blocked her escape from the diner. He hadn't exactly won her over with his what's-in-this-for-you comment but he'd figured once she read his card, she'd be calling as soon as the newspaper opened. People loved to see their names in print. Businesses loved free publicity. He was willing to offer her both.

If she'd call back.

At three o'clock, he fished a local phone book out of the drawer and circled a number. Lakeshore Community Fellowship. Connor talked to a very nice lady and jotted down a name and address before he snapped his cell phone closed. A slow, predatory smile crossed his face.

Sarah Kendle. 314 North Jackson.

Which just happened to be kitty-corner from the newspaper.

Sarah was in the back room, up to her elbows in packing peanuts, when the doorbells announced a customer. With Christmas only a few weeks away, she was officially behind schedule. Giving the cup of tea steeping on her desk a longing look, she hopped over a cardboard box on her way to the front of the store.

"What kind of place is this?"

Sarah frowned, trying to place the voice that rumbled from behind a decorative panel. Definitely masculine… definitely familiar…

"Good morning."

Definitely Connor Lawe.

In her shop. Looking more attractive than he had the night before. Not that she'd paid that much attention. Melting snow glistened in tawny brown hair several shades lighter than his skin. No one had a right to be so tan in December. He wore blue jeans and a black leather jacket, unzipped to reveal a pinstriped Oxford shirt that would have looked stuffy on anyone else. Sarah wasn't fooled. It took a lot of money to look that casual.

"What are you doing here?" She normally never greeted potential customers so bluntly, but she had a strong hunch Connor Lawe wasn't looking for anything Memory Lane carried.

There was only one thing a reporter with his reputation would search for like an overzealous bloodhound. A story. Except that didn't make sense. From what she'd heard about him, his specialty was stirring up controversy, exposing government corruption and ruffling political feathers. So why was he back in town? And why had he bothered to track her to her shop?

"What is all this stuff?" Connor bent down and scooped up a handful of rubber stamps from a wicker bin. "Do people actually buy these things?"

A soft answer turns away wrath. And, hopefully, irritating reporters. "They're stamps."

"For what?"

"Scrapbooking. That's what Memory Lane is. A store that sells scrapbooking supplies."

"Scrap…" Connor's voice trailed off as his gaze scoured the room, coming to rest on the colorful baskets hanging from an antique coatrack Sarah had found in the attic after she'd bought the building.

"…booking," Sarah finished, realizing she was going to have to clarify. "It's a hobby."

"A hobby?"

Sarah fought a sudden urge to smile. Obviously she was witnessing a rare occurrence. Connor Lawe at a loss for words. The befuddled look in his eyes made him seem more…human.

"Scrapbooking is very popular. It's creative—and personal. People can keep it as simple or as detailed as they want it to be, but the result is a keepsake photo album. An heirloom. And it's better for your pictures than shoving them into a shoebox."

"I'll have to take your word for that." Now he was

studying her. As though Memory Lane were a petri dish and she the strange, unidentifiable organism swimming around inside of it. Just when she was tempted to squirm under the scrutiny of those intense gray eyes, she remembered that *he* was on *her* turf. Maybe it was time to start asking *him* some questions.

She took a deep breath. "So, if you aren't looking for some cute background papers for your vacation photos, why are you here?"

"You're kidding me, right? Cute kids dressed like angels who deliver sentimental messages and then top them off with a Christmas carol? If I were a major stockholder in a tissue company, I couldn't have come up with a better angle than this for the Christmas issue."

"No." It was the only word Sarah managed to squeak out around the knot that suddenly formed in her throat.

Connor frowned. "What do you mean *no*?"

Sarah took a deep breath, reminding herself the word *no* probably wasn't familiar to Connor. "There is no *angle*. The girls came up with this idea and I'm not about to let you put your *slant* on it."

"What exactly is my slant?" He picked up a heart-shaped paper punch and tested it.

"You know. That we have some kind of ulterior motive. Like hoping people will make a special donation to the church. Or using the Good News-grams to increase attendance at the Christmas Eve service…"

"Actually, those things hadn't crossed my mind." He pulled a palm-sized notebook out of his pocket and scribbled something down.

Ack. That backfired. Somehow, she had to persuade

him to give up the idea of writing a story about the girls. Roscoe's reaction to his Good News-gram proved that beneath a gruff exterior, a squishy marshmallow heart might be beating. Maybe all she needed to do was appeal to Connor's soft side…

"The girls were nervous last night and to tell you the truth, their parents are a little concerned about them doing this in the first place. I don't think an interview would be a good idea." Everything she said was the truth. Hopefully it would be enough to change his mind.

Connor looked thoughtful. "I don't plan to interview them—"

The relief Sarah felt was cut off as the doorbells jingled cheerfully, announcing another customer. Mrs. Owens. Shrouded from head to toe in a faux leopard-print coat and matching hat, with a large envelope tucked under one arm. The elderly woman was one of the pillars of the community. She was also one of Sarah's best customers, even though she'd never risk her French manicure by picking up a pair of decorative-edged scissors. She hired Sarah to do that for her.

"Sarah. I found 1960 to 1975. Oh my goodness. The *hairstyles.*" Mrs. Owens shuddered delicately. "Atrocious. It's a good thing Jackie made hats fashionable. Saved us all from complete embarrassment."

Connor watched their exchange in fascination. Sarah wouldn't have been surprised to find out he had a miniature tape recorder in his pocket. *All the better to hear you with, my dear.*

"I'll start working on them right away," Sarah promised. "I'm just finishing up your wedding photos—"

"Mrs. Owens." Connor's husky voice suddenly invaded their conversation. "You haven't changed a bit."

Mrs. Owens turned and gasped his name in delight. "*Connor.* Dear boy. Your father mentioned you were coming home for Christmas. From what he tells us at the club, it sounds like you've worn a path around the world. I see you've met our Sarah. Sweet girl. Moved to town a few years ago, during the downtown renovation. She's been organizing all the Owens family photos."

I'm standing right here, Mrs. Owens. Sarah bit the inside of her lip to keep from laughing. Her gaze briefly tangled with Connor's and she was stunned to see an answering spark of humor in his eyes. The moment of connection between them left Sarah unexpectedly breathless.

"I'm sure you have things to do, Mr. Lawe." She had to get rid of him. Her peace of mind depended on it.

"So formal, you two!" Mrs. Owens scolded. "I have to meet Harold for dinner at five, so I'll look at the photos later, Sarah." She patted Sarah's arm and then lifted her chin and blew Connor air kisses—one for each sunwashed cheek. "I'm so glad you're back. Your father misses you, you know. It's about time you took over the business so he can retire."

Mrs. Owens swept out of the shop but Connor stood frozen in place, his gaze fixed on the artificial Christmas tree near the window overlooking The Avenue.

"You're taking over *The Jackson Lake News*?" Sarah finally broke the silence. She tried not to think about what it would mean to see *him* at the monthly chamber of commerce meetings.

"I don't know where she got that idea." His eyes narrowed. "I didn't come back to take over the newspaper. I came back to convince my father to sell it."

He strode toward the door but just before he reached it, he turned and looked at her.

"I'll see you tonight, *Miss Kendle*." His tone gently mocked the formal way she'd addressed him in front of Mrs. Owens. "624 Bonnie Lane. Number 12, right?"

He'd just recited the address of their next Good News-gram delivery.

Sarah's mouth went dry. "How did you know that?"

"Your pastor told me the address when I called him this afternoon. That would have been right after he gave me permission to accompany you and the girls when they deliver the messages." He slipped the notebook into his pocket and had the audacity to wink at her. "Not everyone shuns free publicity, you know."

Chapter Four

"Christmas carols are for old fogies. We should do a rap instead," Mandi announced from the backseat of the church van as it headed toward Bonnie Lane. "What do you guys think?"

Sarah glanced in the rearview mirror just in time to see Jennifer and Alyssa put their heads together for a quick consultation. Judging from the expressions on their faces, the decision was Christmas carols 2, rap 0.

"I even made one up." Mandi began to slap her hands against her knees in an uneven rhythm. "Do you want to hear it?"

"Um…sure." Emma gulped the word.

"Hey, all you shepherds, gather up your flocks. Head to Bethlehem to see a king that *rocks*…"

Sarah knew she had less than a mile to pull together a decent argument as to why traditional carols were the best way to go. Unfortunately, her ability to sway someone to her way of thinking had been put to the test earlier that afternoon during a meeting with Pastor Phillips and the outcome hadn't been very successful.

It was all *his* fault.

Not Pastor Phillips. Connor Lawe.

Right after she'd closed the shop, she'd headed over to the church to talk to Pastor Phillips. On the way there, she'd compiled a short list of reasons—reasonable reasons—why it wouldn't be a good idea for Connor to follow the girls while they made their deliveries.

Number 1. She'd spent a precious hour of her afternoon scanning some of his articles on the internet. Not only did Connor Lawe *not* believe in faith, hope and love, he was deeply suspicious of anyone who did. Which definitely made her and the girls a target for his poison pen.

Number 2. The Good News-grams were meant to be personal. Private. A message to a loved one. Even though they'd sometimes have to deliver them in a public place, doing so under Connor's critical eye would steal something special from the moment.

Number 3. He gave her the jitters.

Sarah had mentally scratched that one off the list. She couldn't confess to her pastor that Connor Lawe played havoc with her senses like a lightning bolt strike to a circuit board. She didn't understand it herself. One minute she felt sorry for him—his career exposed the dark side of mankind while hers celebrated its goodness—and the next minute she wanted to shake the arrogance out of him.

Pastor Phillips had listened while she pleaded her case. One of the things she respected most about Lakeshore Fellowship's personable young pastor was his

James 1:19 personality. *Everyone should be quick to listen, slow to speak and slow to become angry.*

He listened to her pour out her reasons and when he finally did speak, Sarah realized she needed to work on planting that particular verse in her heart. Again. Because Pastor Phillips's reasons turned out to be just as reasonable as hers.

Nothing happens by coincidence or accident, Sarah. Maybe someone will pick up a copy of the News and their life will be touched by Connor's article. Or it might challenge someone to reach out to someone they've been estranged from. Or give them the courage to say "I love you."

How could she argue with that?

In the end, she gave in. Fortunately, when she'd stopped by the church to pick up the girls, there was no sign of Connor. Maybe a scientist had discovered a rare bug in the rainforest and he'd left to get an interview. With the scientist, not the bug.

"Why are you smiling, Sarah?" Emma's voice tugged her back to reality.

"Because she liked my rap. Didn't you, Sarah?" Mandi cast a smug look over her shoulder at Jennifer.

It was time to put the *slow to speak* part of James 1:19 into action.

"You're very creative, Mandi." Sarah chose her words carefully so she wouldn't hurt the girl's feelings. Mandi's mother never made her daughter participate in anything at church other than Wednesday nights, so Sarah was thrilled when Mandi had committed to deliver the Good News-grams with the rest of the girls. She didn't want to do anything to discourage her. "I think we should sing 'O Little Town of Bethlehem' tonight. According to the woman who hired us, it's her dad's favorite Christmas carol."

Mandi disappeared into the sheepskin lining of her jacket until only her eyebrows were visible.

"But maybe you can teach us the words so we can sing it another time." Alyssa's enthusiastic prompt brought an echo of agreement from Emma and Jennifer.

Mandi's nose emerged. Her muffled "okay" allowed Sarah to breathe again. The girls looked out for each other. They were getting it. The thought warmed her more than a cup of hot chocolate.

"Here we are." Sarah eased the unwieldy church van to the side of the street and turned off the engine.

None of the girls moved.

Sarah frowned, taking in their surroundings for the first time. Bonnie Lane split in half at the city limits. To the west, the road traced the picturesque shore of Jackson Lake. To the east, it rolled past the gravel pit to a mobile-home court that had sprouted from an abandoned tract of farmland.

The moonlight cast an eerie blue glow on the snow-capped roofs of the houses and the spindly trees that shuddered in the wind.

"It's kind of creepy," Jennifer whispered.

Mandi snorted but didn't seem to be in a hurry to jump out of the van, either.

"Jennifer, you grab the trumpet. It's on the floor behind your seat. Emma and Mandi, your wings are hanging in the garment bag in the back." *Never let them see you sweat*. A good motto for athletes, corporate execs and, Sarah had discovered, youth leaders.

Besides that, she knew better than to judge a book by its cover. Or people by the house they lived in. One of the more conventional dwellings in her gypsy-like childhood had been a rustic cabin in a national park. Some of the more unconventional included a sailboat, a two-person tent and an old lighthouse on the Lake Superior shoreline.

Headlights speared the darkness as a mammoth SUV careened up the street and ground to a stop, spitting up slush and snow only inches from the van's bumper.

Emma pressed her nose against the window. "It's that man again."

When Sarah had picked up the girls at church, she'd told them that a reporter from *The Jackson Lake News* had Pastor Phillips's permission to accompany them that evening. They'd shrieked in delight. Not exactly the response Sarah had been hoping for.

"He's going to write an article about *us*?" Jennifer had asked, immediately fishing a compact mirror out of her patchwork leather purse to check her braces for traces of the red licorice they'd been munching on.

"That's right." *A biased, slanted article about church corruption or blatant heart-tugging plots designed to fill the smiley-face banks in the Sunday schoolrooms.*

She didn't say that, though. It definitely fell into the *slow to become angry* category.

Connor tapped on her window. Sarah opened the door a crack. "I thought you decided not to come." The words were out before Sarah could stop them.

"You mean, you were hoping."

"I don't care what people say. You *are* quick." Sarah clapped a mittened hand over her lips. Obviously she needed to do more than simply memorize James 1:19. She needed to wallpaper her apartment with the verse.

Connor's husky laugh went straight through her. With his guard down, maybe she could try one last time to convince him to find another story to write about. She slipped out of the driver's seat and eased the door closed so the girls couldn't eavesdrop on their conversation.

"The woman who sent us here mentioned that her Dad has been kind of depressed since he retired. I don't think he's going to be comfortable having you sticking a microphone in his face—" Sarah suddenly noticed the camera hanging around his neck "—or taking his picture."

"Everyone likes having their picture taken." Connor shrugged. "You should know that. Your business is built on it, right?" Sarah might have argued the point if he'd given her the chance. "I planned to bring Marcus, the staff photographer, with me, but I decided to take the photos myself."

Hope tweaked her heart. Maybe a sensitive heart did beat under that expensive leather jacket.

"He had a hockey game tonight."

Or maybe not.

Silently, Sarah repeated Pastor Phillips's motto. *No accidents or coincidences with God. No accidents or coincidences with God.*

"I'll fade into the background. You won't even notice I'm there."

Six-foot-two. Broad shoulders, muscular frame. Windswept, toffee-colored hair. Eyes the color of mercury.

Sure she wouldn't.

Connor heard a giggle and noticed the girls standing shoulder to shoulder several yards away. Grinning. He had no experience with kids—especially pre-teen girls—but if he had to guess, he'd say they were up to something.

His gaze moved back to Sarah. She looked adorably frustrated. Probably because her last-ditch effort to get him to scrap the article had crashed and burned. With his eyes, he traced the delicate lines of her face, lingering on the pert nose. He flicked a glance at her left hand. Under that bright red mitten, there had to be a ring.

A woman like Sarah Kendle was the poster child for hearth and home. The quaint touches he'd noticed in her shop—the comfy chairs near the window display and the urn of hot chocolate—encouraged customers to linger. Which meant Sarah was either a shrewd businesswoman who understood that the longer a person stayed, the more money they spent, or she really did want people to feel at home in her store.

So if feathering the proverbial nest was so important to her, why did she choose to spend her evenings traipsing around in the cold with her ragtag group of "angels" to tell people that God loved them and looking like she believed it might really make a difference?

He barely remembered his mother, Natalie, but he

remembered hearing similar platitudes after she died. She'd been a woman of faith, too, but in the end it hadn't been enough to keep her with them. He hadn't only lost her; in the ways that counted, he'd lost his father, too. It was as if Natalie's love had held their family together and when she was gone, silence eventually crept through the house and filled it, leaving no room to breathe. Robert escaped into his work and eventually Connor followed in his footsteps. But he'd escaped from…everything. A house that held only painful memories. A small town that stifled him. And a father who refused to grieve.

And now he was back. Standing ankle-deep in snow. Trying to figure out how to convince his father to sell the business he'd poured his life into. And about to write an article that had the potential to destroy any future relationship with a wide-eyed optimist who sported a crown of untamed auburn curls and offered a generous smile to cranky cooks and tired waitresses.

Connor mentally shook himself. The freezing temperature had not only numbed his toes, it must have numbed his brain. Relationship? The word wasn't in his vocabulary. He'd let his career fill every nook and cranny of his life. There wasn't room for anything—or anyone—else. Especially someone like Sarah Kendle.

His survival instincts kicked in and he retreated into reporter mode. Waving his camera at the girls, he motioned them over. "Can I get a picture before we go inside?"

The carrot-top bounded over to him and the rest of them followed. "I can't find the trumpet, Sarah."

Sarah disappeared into the van again and Connor found himself alone with Sarah's "angels." He'd been in dangerous situations in the past, but something in these bright, curious pairs of eyes sent a shiver of fear up his spine.

"Since I'm going to be following you around for a few weeks, you should tell me your names," Connor suggested.

"Jennifer Sands." The carrot-top spoke up first and gave him an engaging smile, revealing a mouthful of metal. The green and red rubber bands stretched between her braces had obviously been chosen with the holiday season in mind. "This is Emma and Mandi and Alyssa."

Jennifer was the queen bee. The other girls—even the one with the sour expression—huddled around her as if she were a quarterback on Super Bowl Sunday.

Connor relaxed. His imagination must have been playing tricks on him. These were twelve-year-old girls. Even without Sarah's cooperation, they should be easy to manage.

He lifted the camera and adjusted the focus. The girls jiggled and twitched like a litter of puppies. His head started to swim.

"Aren't you going to wait for Sarah?" Jennifer asked.

"Um…" Connor hadn't planned to include Sarah. Behind those calm, Caribbean blue eyes lurked a sense of humor. She'd cross her eyes or stick out her tongue at him. He just knew it.

"She's pretty, isn't she?" Emma blinked up at him. "Um…"

"She's nice, too," Alyssa chimed in.

"And funny." Mandi—who maybe wasn't as moody as he'd thought at first—actually giggled.

"Hold still for just a—"

"Are you married?" Jennifer asked.

The heat that crept into his face melted the snowflakes caught in his eyelashes. "No."

The girls exchanged glances. That peculiar ripple of unease danced through him again.

"Sarah isn't married, either."

"Really." Connor snapped the picture, not even bothering to take another one in case the first one didn't turn out. "All done. It looks like Sarah's waiting for you."

He sighed in relief as they scampered away, holding up the hems of their robes. Laughing as the wind tugged at their halos.

Sarah waited until they reached the door before knocking on it. When it finally opened a crack, an elderly man stood on the other side, resting his weight on a wooden cane.

As if the girls had rehearsed the moment a hundred times, Jennifer stepped forward and raised her arms.

"Do not be afraid. I bring you good news of great joy…"

Chapter Five

The girls huddled together in the back of the van, a quilt thrown over their heads to muffle the sound of their voices. In the front of the vehicle, Sarah hummed the chorus of the carol they'd sung for Mr. Banister.

"Admit it. I'm right." Jennifer crossed her arms over her chest.

Emma caught her lower lip in her teeth. "I don't know."

"Didn't you notice the way they acted around each other?"

"They wouldn't *look* at each other," Mandi pointed out.

"And Sarah seemed kind of mad when she told us he was going to write an article about the Good News-grams."

"Exactly." Jennifer gave her friends a superior smile. "According to my sister, when two people won't look at each other, it's because they *like* each other. Once they start, they won't be able to stop. It's like eating cookie dough. And Janie's in college, so she should know."

The other girls murmured their approval. Jennifer's sister, Janie, did have a lot of boyfriends.

"Sarah does seem lonely," Emma admitted. "I heard my mom say she doesn't have any family."

A moment of silence descended on the group out of respect for Sarah's family status.

"What if they don't *ever* look at each other? Then what?" Mandi asked.

"That's where we come in," Jennifer said, her voice thin with excitement.

"I don't know." Emma peeked around the corner of the quilt and watched the tassel on Sarah's hat bounce in time with "Sleigh Ride." "Maybe Sarah wants to find her own husband."

"They're both about the same age and neither of them is bad looking." Jennifer's shrug displaced the quilt and they yanked it over their heads again. "And you know what Sarah is always telling us."

Their voices blended together as they solemnly recited one of their youth leader's favorite phrases. "God's greatest gift is love."

"And Christmas is, like, the perfect time to give a gift, right? She's not going to always have us around to keep her busy, you know." Jennifer put out her hand. "So who's in?"

Three fingers curled around hers and squeezed.

The high-pitched squeals under the quilt told Sarah she shouldn't have let the girls eat so much of Mr. Banister's homemade fudge. She wasn't going to win a prize for Youth Leader of the Year if she sent four adolescent girls home supercharged with sugar.

She fumbled with the radio and turned down the volume. The windshield wipers went on instead. Maybe they needed to add a new church van to their prayer list. "What's going on back there?"

"Nothing!"

The quick response only convinced her there was. The girls had been acting strange all evening. She'd noticed how quickly they'd taken to Connor. It surprised her because Connor wasn't exactly the warm, teddy-bear type of guy who drew kids like an outdoor jungle gym. Emma, who barely made eye contact with her, didn't seemed to be intimidated by his aloofness. She'd even been brave enough to offer him a piece of fudge. And Mandi, whose negative comments about men hinted at the lingering pain over her parent's divorce, had asked him questions about the countries he'd traveled to.

Sarah had expected Connor to leave right after he got the photo and the information he needed, but instead he'd joined them at the scuffed kitchen table and listened while Mr. Banister, who'd been forced into early retirement by an accident, entertained them with stories of his career as a lumberjack.

Sarah noticed that as the evening progressed, the older man's shoulders lifted from their weary slump and his eyes looked brighter. Even though she hadn't planned to stay longer than it took to deliver the message from Mr. Banister's daughter, Sarah sensed the man needed more than a Christmas carol. He needed laughter. And life. And someone to listen.

When Alyssa had stifled a yawn, Sarah realized she

had to get the girls back to the church. Their parents were scheduled to pick them up at eight o'clock and the next Good News-gram might depend on how long they were forced to wait in the cold parking lot for their daughters!

Mr. Banister had honked loudly into a white handkerchief when the girls danced out the door of his tiny trailer into the darkness.

"Nice kids to give up TV for a night to listen to an old man ramble on," he muttered. "It gets kind of quiet around here at night."

Sarah noticed the hand-carved chess set on the coffee table and had an idea. "Some of the men who attend Lakeshore Community Fellowship formed a chess club last year, Mr. Banister. If you're interested, I'll have the contact person call you. They get together once a week to play chess and have coffee. You might enjoy it."

Mr. Banister cleared his throat. "Wouldn't hurt, I suppose."

Without thinking, Sarah had leaned over and kissed the man's weathered cheek. When she'd turned, she collided with Connor's cool gaze.

"A chess club, huh?" He murmured as she brushed past him. "I'll bet a person has to pay dues to belong."

"It's a good thing I don't bet, then, because you'd lose," Sarah had said.

Frustrating man.

Replaying their conversation, she almost missed the turnoff to the church parking lot. As the girls tumbled out of the van, Sarah joined them to close the evening in prayer.

"I'll see you on Saturday at noon. That's our next delivery," Sarah told them.

"Is Mr. Lawe going to be there?" Jennifer asked.

Sarah forced a smile. "I'm sure he will be."

As the girls hurried to meet up with their parents, Sarah heard Jennifer say something to Emma that sounded suspiciously like, "See, I told you so."

When Connor got back to his father's house, he found Robert asleep on the couch. His dad looked more fragile than Connor had ever seen him. He looked… old. Deep lines scored his face, his hair had thinned and even summer weekends on the golf course hadn't erased the pallor that resulted from a weakening heart.

Robert Lawe had always been a force to be reckoned with—a man who seemed larger than life—but for the first time Connor didn't see a man he had to prove something to. He just saw…a man. A man battling advancing years and failing health. *His father.*

You've been gone too long.

The words crept in as Connor stared down at Robert.

No. He couldn't have stayed in Jackson Lake. Robert hadn't *wanted* him to. Like in an old Western, the town just wasn't big enough for the both of them. Connor's lips twisted. Eventually they would have faced off in a showdown on The Avenue.

Maybe that showdown was yet to come.

Connor still felt the fallout from the bomb Alice Owens had dropped on him in Sarah's shop. *It's about time you take over the business so your father can retire.*

Give up the career he'd spent the last decade building to rusticate in his hometown? *The Jackson Lake News* was a dinosaur. A weekly newspaper that still published recipes and local gossip.

"You home, son?" Robert's eyes fluttered open and focused on him. Blurry. Confused.

Son.

"Were you waiting up for me, Dad?" Connor had to crack a joke to offset the sudden burning behind his eyes.

Robert pushed himself into a sitting position and began to search his pockets. Connor spotted his father's glasses on the side table but knew better than to point them out. His dad accepted help like a cat accepted a knot in its tail.

"I must have fallen asleep. Who can stay awake during all those commercials?" Robert grumbled. "Where've you been? It's after eight."

"Past my curfew, huh?" Connor grinned, dropped in the chair opposite the sofa and propped his feet on the coffee table. "As a matter of fact, I was working on an assignment from my editor."

"What assignment?"

"A warm fuzzy Christmas story, remember?"

"What did you find?" Robert's eyebrows met in the center of his forehead. "Shop with a Cop? It's been done. Mittens from the Mission Circle? Last year's news."

Connor noticed the chess set on the marble side table by the fireplace and remembered the expression on Mr. Banister's face when Sarah mentioned the group of men who got together to play. She certainly seemed to have a way with people. Unlike him.

"Trust me. This one is new. I happened to be in the right place at the right time." Connor nodded at the chess set. "Are you up to a game?"

"Chess? I'll beat you and you'll cry again."

"Dad, I was ten years old the last time we played. I promise I won't cry this time if you win."

Robert shrugged. "I don't have anything better to do."

As a teenager, the gruff response would have sent Connor out of the room to follow his own pursuits. He'd refused to waste time with someone who didn't want him around. This time, he decided to stay and see what would happen.

He stood up and caught the flash of regret in Robert's eyes. The one he would have missed if he'd simply walked away like he'd done in the past.

Was it possible his dad was getting tired of the tension between them, too?

Maybe for the second time, he was in the right place at the right time. Sarah Kendle would probably call it divine intervention. He called it a coincidence.

Sarah peered through the row of corkscrew curls that formed a curtain over her eyes, keeping an eye on the customer stalking around the shop. The one whose broad shoulders barely cleared the narrow aisle between the displays.

He was back. Again. Sarah had hoped he'd sleep in on Saturday morning and skip the Good News-gram the girls were scheduled to deliver.

No such luck.

When he'd walked in minutes after she unlocked the door, she'd given herself a paper cut. Then she'd nicked her finger on a pair of scissors. Not only did Connor's presence inflict serious damage on her peace of mind, if he stayed in her shop any longer, she'd be a patient at the walk-in clinic by noon.

Connor paused to stare at a framed photograph on the wall. There were several, but she could tell by his position which one had captured his attention. A close-up of a bull moose. A slice of light from the morning sun captured every glistening bead of water that fell from the animal's muzzle as it lifted its head from the river.

"Is this an Anne Elliott?"

Sarah's breath caught in her throat and she tried another one. A little bit better. "Yes."

Connor had his back to her as he studied the photograph. "I bought five photos from her Maine collection. I don't have this one." He sounded a little put out.

Sarah suppressed a smile. "It's not part of the *Maine* series. That one was taken on Isle Royale in Lake Superior."

Connor tossed a frown over his shoulder, clearly skeptical. "Are you sure? I collect her work and I've never seen this one."

"I'm sure." Humor threaded Sarah's voice as she stepped around the counter and came over to stand beside him. "I was with her when she took it."

She was serious.

And suddenly Connor saw it. The faint resemblance to the woman whose face graced the book jacket of his first edition printing of Anne Elliott's Winter collection. The piquant chin. The large, wide-spaced eyes. The women were too far apart in age to be sisters, the resemblance too uncanny to be anything less than immediate family. "Anne Elliott is your *mother*?"

"Was." Sarah wouldn't look at him. "She died two years ago from ovarian cancer."

"I'm sorry." The words sounded inadequate even to Connor's ears. And judging from the rigid set of Sarah's shoulders, he'd inadvertently scraped against a wound that hadn't healed. "I hadn't heard. I keep tabs on what's going on in the world but sometimes I lose track of what's happening in my own backyard."

"Not many people know. It's the way she wanted it. Mom never liked drawing attention to herself." Sarah's lips tilted. "All she wanted to do was snap pictures. Becoming famous surprised her."

"There's another book scheduled for release this spring, if I remember correctly." He'd preordered it the year before and had wondered about the two year lapse between collections.

Sarah nodded. "Her publisher just finished her last collection. It's not as complete as her early work, but they included some of her journal entries this time. And there'll be a tribute to her in the front."

Sarah didn't say so, but Connor knew she'd written it. It was obvious that she and her mother had been close. The urge to wrap his arms around Sarah and absorb some of her pain shocked him. He stuck his hands in his pockets. Just to keep them in line.

"You said you were with her when this was taken?"

Sarah's gaze moved to the photo. She chucked softly. "He surprised us more than we surprised him. Mom didn't usually photograph wildlife, that's why it didn't end up in a book. But she wore her camera like a necklace, so she never missed an opportunity to take a picture. She lived behind the lens."

The undercurrent in Sarah's voice made him curious. "Did you travel with her a lot?"

"Up until two years ago." Sarah pivoted and started to walk away. "Would you like to see more of her work? Mom was a perfectionist. I rescued dozens of photos from the wastebasket over the years."

Strangely enough, Connor suddenly found himself more interested in Sarah's childhood than in the unpublished photos of legendary photographer Anne Elliott.

Chapter Six

Sarah retrieved an album from behind the counter and her slim fingers smoothed the surface of the soft leather cover before she slid it over to him.

Connor lingered over each page, aware of Sarah's eyes on him. She was probably as shocked to find out he was a fan of her mother's work as he was to discover the daughter of an award-winning nature photographer living in sleepy little Jackson Lake. "I can't see anything wrong with these. The light. The composition. They're all perfect."

"I think so, too, but if Mom were here, she'd be able to point out the flaws."

Connor's emotions stirred as he stared at several images of the Rockies. Anne Elliott's signature style captured slices of changing landscapes around the country. She worked only in black and white—each photo as stark as a pen and ink drawing, and etched with a haunting loneliness. He'd always been amazed that a photographer could coax such emotion out of the landscape.

"She loved the mountains, didn't she?"

"She did. Mom liked to say the plains were God's living room, but the mountains were His library."

Anne Elliott's career spanned thirty years—he had several rare prints of her early work—so Sarah must have grown up roaming the United States. The most isolated, desolate parts of it. The reality didn't fit with his first impressions of hearth-and-home Sarah.

"Did you enjoy traveling with—" He finally voiced the question that had been nagging him since he'd started paging through the album, but the bells over the door drowned out the rest of his words.

"Excuse me." Sarah slipped past him to greet a customer.

Connor went behind the counter to put the album away and noticed another one on the shelf. This one covered in blue dime-store plastic. He pulled it out and flipped through it.

It wasn't Anne's work. No black and white. No fragile wildflowers or lacy ferns or jagged rocks. The photos were in color. And all the subjects were people. A tiny Native American boy, with fathomless chocolate-brown eyes, dressed in a ceremonial costume trimmed in scarlet and sapphire-blue. A cowboy hunched over a campfire, the steam from his first cup of coffee beading his leathery skin.

They took his breath away.

"What are you doing?" Sarah practically snatched the album out of his hands.

"Have you shown these?"

Sarah's face paled, darkening her eyes to the blue of a winter storm. "How do you know they're mine?"

Gut instinct? Connor pried her fingers off the album and opened it again, paging through it as Sarah stood next to him, taut as a bowstring. "Your mother never photographed people."

"No. She didn't find people fascinating. Or worthy of her attention. She saw God in His creation—that's what she wanted to get across to people. I'm probably the only photographer's child who doesn't have any baby pictures."

Connor listened for bitterness but heard only affection. "What did she think of your work?"

Sarah laughed. "It wasn't my *work*—it was a hobby. We'd be out on a shoot for months at a time. I picked up a camera one day just for fun and took pictures of some children on the Hopi reservation. It helped pass the time. Mom always told me I was better at scrap-booking pictures than taking them."

Her mother was wrong.

Connor saw real talent in Sarah's photos. They differed from Anne's in style and technique, but not quality. For reasons he didn't want to analyze, he couldn't let Sarah think her photos were inferior.

"You just said your mother wanted people to see God through His creation?" Connor didn't wait for Sarah to answer. "Your photos express the same thing in a different way. God created man, didn't He?"

Sarah stared at him as if the idea had never occurred to her. And maybe it hadn't. "You believe in God?"

"Don't put words in my mouth." It figured. She by-passed the compliment and zeroed in to search for a deeper meaning in his words. What she'd discover would disappoint her. Covering the news in the world's hot spots for the last decade had strip-mined his soul. "I'm not saying He doesn't exist, I just don't think He intervenes in people's lives here on little old earth."

He waited, expecting Sarah to launch into one of the familiar, defensive arguments he'd heard from people like her in the past.

She didn't. Her silence didn't make sense. She was a believer. Wasn't she obligated to refute statements like the one he'd just made.

"Connor! Just the man I was hoping to see today." Alice Owens' voice trilled above the bells. Chanel No. 5 surfed in on a gust of December wind. "When I was sorting through my photo boxes yesterday, I found this one of your mother. I thought you might like to have it. Such a beauty, our Natalie. With a voice like an angel. I think half the people who came to the Christmas Eve service at church came just to hear her sing 'O Holy Night.'"

Connor's throat closed as Mrs. Owens tugged a photo out of her purse.

"I don't remember." He tucked the photo in his coat pocket without looking at it.

But suddenly…he did.

The memory stirred inside him. He remembered wriggling around on the hard church pew, sneaking a bite of the candy cane the usher had given him. Hearing his dad mutter under his breath about the length of the service. And he remembered his mother, standing at the front of the church, wearing a green velvet dress. Singing.

The walls of Sarah's shop began to shrink around him.

"I have another appointment, but I'll see you at noon, Sarah. And Mrs. Owens, thank you for the photo. I'll give it to Dad." Even though it would end up in the mysterious place all the other photos of Natalie had gone.

He took several steps toward the door but Sarah called him back. "Connor?"

Hearing his name stopped Connor in his tracks. It was the first time Sarah dropped the formal Mr. Lawe and called him by his first name.

"Here." She lifted the Isle Royale photo off the wall and handed it to him. When he realized she was *giving* it to him, he tried to press it back into her hands. She wouldn't take it.

"I can't accept this."

"You like it, it's yours. Consider it an early Christmas present."

"Sarah…" He didn't know what to say. Was she trying to soften him up so he wouldn't accompany her and the girls? Or had she seen his reaction to the photo of Natalie and felt sorry for him? Neither reason set well. Overwhelmed by the generous gesture even as he rejected it, he let his inner cynic loose. "You know I don't believe in Christmas. Everyone acknowledges Jesus wasn't really born on December twenty-fifth."

She didn't take offense. Nor did she snatch the photo from his unworthy hands.

"Maybe the *when* of Christmas isn't as important as the *why*."

On the way to Mason Street, Sarah couldn't forget the expression on Connor's face when she'd given him the picture. Disbelief. Suspicion.

You'd think no one had ever given him a gift before, Lord.

She brought her complaint to God in prayer, knowing His gentle nudge against her soul had been what prompted her to give the photo to Connor in the first place.

Instead of being warmed by the spirit of giving, he'd looked at her as if she'd offered him a package with an audible tick!

He's as cold as one of those icicles hanging off the roof, God. It makes me wonder what kind of article he's writing about us....

"Sarah! You missed the turn." Jennifer shouted from the backseat.

Sighing, Sarah aimed the van into the nearest driveway and turned it around. Bev, the waitress from Roscoe's Diner, had called her to set up their Saturday morning delivery. Bev couldn't share many details about Francine, the new dishwasher, other than she'd been forced to get a job after her husband had left her.

"Don't tell her I'm the one who sent you," Bev had said. "I'm not one to get mixed up in other people's business, but I got to thinking one of those songs might cheer her up a little bit. She's got a tough row to hoe."

Sarah switched off the ignition and glanced at her watch as a black SUV bore down on them. Right on time. Connor Lawe might be a Scrooge, but he was a punctual one. Armed and dangerous with a camera around his neck and a tape recorder in his pocket.

"Hi, Mr. Lawe." The girls chimed his name together sweetly.

Sarah resisted the urge to roll her eyes as she lined the angels up for a quick inspection. She straightened Mandi's wings, re-pinned the back of Emma's robe and adjusted Alyssa's halo. She glanced down at the four pairs of gold boots and decided another coat of spray paint was in order.

"Trumpet?"

"Check."

"CD player?"

"Check."

"Jennifer, did you pick out a song?"

"Uh-huh. 'Silent Night.'"

"I still think we should do the rap instead," Mandi muttered.

Two inches of snow had fallen during the night, dusting the uneven concrete sidewalk leading to the front door. There were no signs of life and Sarah hoped the woman wasn't still asleep. According to Bev, Francine wasn't scheduled to work at the diner until later that afternoon.

Masking tape crisscrossed the rusty doorbell so she peeled off her glove and rapped on the door as the girls clustered behind her, using her as a windbreak.

When it opened, a young woman stood on the other side. Her arms cradled an infant while two older children wearing footed pajamas—with the feet cut out—clung to her legs.

"Is Francine Carmichael here?" Sarah asked, sure she'd somehow gotten the address wrong. For some reason, she'd assumed the woman would be older.

"I'm Francine." The woman's eyes widened when

the girls peeked around Sarah and then she frowned. "If you're selling something, you'll have to come back some other time. I'm flat broke right now."

"We're here to deliver a Good News-gram." Jennifer lifted the trumpet, eyed the sleeping baby and lowered it again with a grin. "Can we come in? It's cold out here."

"I don't know…" Francine's gaze flicked to Sarah, who gave her a reassuring smile.

"We're here to deliver a message. From a friend. It'll only take a few minutes."

"All right." Francine shrugged one slim shoulder and let them pass. Connor was the last one in line and Sarah noticed the camera had disappeared. Before she had time to wonder about it, they were in Francine's tiny living room. And Sarah came face to face with a kind of poverty she'd naively assumed didn't exist in a town like Jackson Lake.

The couch, still layered with an assortment of pillows and blankets, obviously doubled as a bed for either Francine or the children. A colorful sheet had been creatively strung from light fixture to light fixture, bisecting the room into two separate living areas. One side, a mock-up of a dining room, contained a card table, folding metal chairs and a high chair. The other side had been turned into a makeshift nursery with a crib and changing table.

Jennifer raised her arms. "Do not be afraid. I bring you good news of great joy that will be for all the people. Today in the town of David a Savior has been born; He is Christ, the Lord."

During the recitation, Francine's daughter had sidled

closer to Emma to inspect her wings while the boy tried to wrestle the trumpet away from Mandi, who finally gave in and let him take it.

Distracted by the charming antics, Sarah almost missed her cue to turn the CD player on.

As the last words of "Silent Night" echoed around the room, the baby in Francine's arms stirred and opened its eyes.

Silence. Mandi stepped on Jennifer's toe and Jennifer gave a tiny yelp.

"This Good News-gram is to tell you that God loves you and so does…" Jennifer paused and glanced at Sarah, her eyes wide with panic. Because Bev had asked to remain anonymous, Sarah hadn't given the girls a name. She ad-libbed. "So do we."

Francine burst into tears.

The four girls looked at Sarah in horror. Connor, standing just inside the door, took a step forward.

Sarah didn't stop to think. She crossed the distance between them and gently took the baby from Francine and deposited her into Emma's waiting arms. She drew Francine to the couch and wrapped her arms around the young woman, hugging her until the worst of her inner storm subsided.

"I don't know why he…left," Francine choked. "Everything is a mess. We're all alone…"

Sarah took a deep breath. "No, you're not."

Chapter Seven

"They didn't have a tree."

Emma's words broke the weighted silence that had fallen over the girls on the way back to the church.

"Or lights."

"Or *presents*." The disbelief in Mandi's voice would have made Sarah smile if the reality of the Carmichaels' situation hadn't been so heartbreaking.

She'd tried to comfort Francine, but wasn't sure if she'd succeeded. The vacant look in the young mother's eyes reminded Sarah of photos she'd seen of women living in war-ravaged countries. After she'd prayed with her, Francine had managed a smile and thanked them for coming, but Sarah had a hunch the moment of brightness the girls had brought to the family's day would fade as soon as they left.

It hadn't helped to find Connor waiting for her by the van.

"When is your next appointment?"

The dispassionate question left her feeling as barren as the Carmichael home.

Sarah couldn't understand his lack of emotion. She'd chanced a quick look at him while Francine cried in her arms but he'd seemed unmoved by the woman's tears. At least, Sarah thought bitterly, he hadn't peppered Francine with questions or taken pictures.

"I have to check the calendar."

The expression on his face told her he knew she was purposely being difficult. "Fine. You have my card."

Instead of telling him it was in the wastebasket, Sarah had silently recited James 1:19. The verse she'd forever associate with Connor Lawe.

"Can't we do something for them, Sarah?" Mandi begged, pulling Sarah back to reality. "Like get them a Christmas tree or something? The house was so… gloomy."

God loves you.

Connor had repeated the words in a low voice and then punched his final thought home before striding back to his car.

It's too bad platitudes won't pay the family's heat bill this winter, isn't it?

Connor's cynical observation cycled back through Sarah's mind as the rest of the girls grabbed onto Mandi's suggestion and began to brainstorm ways they could bring Christmas to the Carmichaels.

She knew what he'd say about the idea. Christmas trees and presents wouldn't fill a gap created by a missing husband and father. Or keep food on the table. Or heal a broken heart.

But maybe they'd convince Francine that people

cared about her. That she wasn't alone. That God *did* love her.

"Call your parents," Sarah said firmly. "Ask them if it's all right if I keep you the rest of the afternoon."

Sarah saw the cars lined up on the road and realized half the population of Jackson Lake must have decided Saturday was the perfect day to drive out to Penny Whistle Farm and cut down a Christmas tree.

Armed with a saw, the girls decided to ride in the horse-drawn wagon to the cider house after they picked out a tree. Sarah panted to keep up with them as they waded through ankle-deep snow into the plantation.

The girls dismissed tree after tree. Spruce. Balsam. Pine. One was too spindly. One was too short. Jennifer even declared one the "wrong shade of green."

Sarah silently vowed never to take them shopping.

"How about that one?" Jennifer pointed to a postcard-perfect Fraser fir in a section marked off with yellow tape.

Sarah took a silent inventory of her wallet and decided the tree was worth a week of eating pasta. "I'll cut it down. Saws are for youth workers only."

The girls spotted some classmates and ran off as Sarah knelt down in the snow and began to hack away at the thick trunk.

The soft, comforting jingle of the horse's harness mingled with the laughter of children trudging behind their parents. Sarah closed her eyes for a moment, absorbing the sound. Penny Whistle Farm, offering hot chocolate capped with whipped cream, steaming apple cider and sleigh rides, was considered a family outing, but Sarah had turned the five-mile trip into an annual sojourn since moving to Jackson Lake. Anne's career had made it difficult to develop holiday traditions and even though Sarah wouldn't trade her unconventional childhood for a more traditional one, she embraced the things most people took for granted.

Most years, she and her mother hadn't had a living room, let alone a Christmas tree. The year Sarah turned twelve, Christmas dinner had consisted of fresh salmon grilled over an open fire in an isolated village in Alaska. The following year, they'd spent Christmas Eve basking in the sun on the deck of a sloop off the coast of California.

Sarah hadn't complained. Even though Anne's work consumed most of her time and energy, they were a team. It wasn't until Sarah reached her late teens that she began to long for roots. To live in a familiar place with familiar people. She never expressed that secret yearning to Anne—not even during those final months when her mother's health steadily declined and they spent hours sitting together on the porch of the cabin one of Anne's colleagues had loaned them. But somehow, Anne had known. After she passed away, her attorney had given Sarah the key to a safety deposit box. It took three months for Sarah to muster the strength to open it. When she did, she found a bank book and a letter.

You always encouraged my dreams, now it's time for yours to come true.

So Sarah came back to live in a town she'd seen only

once. On the way to Isle Royale, she and Anne had stopped in Jackson Lake to buy groceries. While Anne, with her usual single-minded determination, conquered the deli, Sarah had wandered down the Avenue and imagined living and working in one of the quaint brick buildings along the tree-lined street. In July, there'd be a parade with a caravan of patriotic floats and dozens of miniature flags. In December, festive window displays and greenery. But most of all, there'd be people whose faces were *familiar*. She wouldn't have to take their pictures to remember them—she'd see them every day. She'd know their names and how many children they had. What kind of cars they drove. What they did for a living…

Out of all the places they'd traveled, Jackson Lake became engraved in her heart that day. Somehow, it had come to represent *home* to Sarah. She'd never forgotten it. And now, she couldn't imagine leaving it.

Why had Connor?

Once again Sarah's thoughts drifted—as they did with frustrating frequency—to Jackson Lake's award-winning journalist. Given Robert's fragile health, Connor would be the logical choice to take his father's place at the helm of *The Jackson Lake News*. It wouldn't be a big leap from reporter to editor. But judging from the expression on Connor's face when he'd said he'd come back to sell the newspaper, the logical choice hadn't occurred to him.

He was probably like Anne. With an entire world to explore, putting down roots, especially in a small town like Jackson Lake, would be the equivalent of being clamped in chains. In a month, he'd be bored covering city council meetings and interviewing the Resident of the Month at the local nursing home.

She couldn't think of anything that would convince a man like Connor Lawe—a man at the peak of his career—to trade the life he was living for a life of stability. And predictability.

Why was the thought so depressing? It didn't matter to her what Connor chose to do with his life.

Deliberately, she pushed her thoughts down a different track. The Carmichaels. Not only did the girls plan to give the family a tree but they also wanted to be involved in decorating it. And they wanted to talk to Pastor Phillips about making sure there were presents under it on Christmas morning.

She was so proud of the girls. She hadn't realized the Good News-grams would become more than delivering a message, and they'd become an opportunity to serve. In spite of what Connor thought, they weren't simply telling people like Francine that God loves them. They were finding ways to *show* it.

Connor. The man derailed her thoughts once again. Unwittingly, even thinking about him had made her attack the tree trunk with a vengeance. Wood chips flew through the air like confetti and the joints in her fingers began to protest.

Sarah sighed and relaxed her grip on the saw. The tool might have been a butter knife considering the amount of progress she was making!

"Can I give you a hand with that?"

A masculine voice penetrated the thick wool cap she

wore and Sarah tilted her head back to smile at her rescuing knight in shining…flannel.

Connor.

From a distance, Connor had seen the woman struggling to chop down a towering Fraser with a saw that probably outweighed her.

He'd already spent more time at the tree farm than he'd intended, but a surge of chivalry had urged him down the snowy footpath to offer his assistance.

The last face he'd expected to see smiling up at him was Sarah's. The wind had kissed her nose and cheeks a rosy pink, enhancing the blue-green eyes.

"What are *you* doing here?" Her smile faded.

"I…um." Did he have to tell her? "I'm writing an article about how wasteful it is to cut down perfectly healthy trees just for the sake of tradition?"

A reluctant smile tugged at the corners of Sarah's lips. She didn't believe him? He was losing his touch.

He squatted down and held out his hand. "Saw."

"Yes, Doctor."

"They have people running around all over the place to cut down trees, you know."

"What would be the fun in that?" Sarah tried to wedge a stray curl under her hat and two more slipped free.

What, indeed?

In less than ten seconds the tree hit the ground, sending a spray of powdery snow into the air.

"Thank you."

The chill in Sarah's voice clued him into the fact

she'd remembered his comments at the Carmichael's house.

Not that he blamed her.

His conscience twisted, no longer dormant. He blamed Jackson Lake. The town was like a bad case of frostbite. No, that wasn't quite true. It was more like the *after*effects of frostbite. When the numbness wears away and those first tingles begin. Like a thousand hot needles jabbed into soft skin. It made a person think they were dying but what was really happening was… life.

The sooner he left town, the better. He wasn't used to feeling. In order to do his job well, he'd learned to shut down his emotions. After a while, it became easier not to let himself feel at all. He didn't need old memories prying open the places he'd sealed off. He'd managed to walk away from Jackson Lake once without looking back. He could do it again.

"Mr. Lawe! Mr. Lawe!"

Connor held his ground as a breathless quartet charged toward him. To flinch would have been a sign of weakness.

"What are you doing here?"

He neatly sidestepped that question again with one of his own. A sneaky but effective maneuver he'd learned in the field. "Is this your tree?"

"Isn't it awesome?" Jennifer grinned and the sun sparked off her braces. "I picked it out."

"We better get going." Sarah grabbed one of the lower branches of the tree and pulled. It didn't budge. "A little help here, girls!"

He buried a sigh. "Do you want—"

"We'll manage." Sarah cut him off.

The four girls positioned themselves on either side of the tree and burrowed through the branches to find one that would make a sturdy handle. Alyssa yelped when the needles poked through her mitten. Emma's scarf somehow got tangled with Mandi's. To Connor, it looked like a recipe for disaster but he had his own reasons for not butting in.

"Aren't you coming back to the warming house for cider, Mr. Lawe?" Jennifer asked as they finally hefted the tree and marched past him.

"I don't think so."

"But—"

"We'll have to take ours to go," Sarah interrupted. "We have a lot to do this afternoon."

The girls lapsed into silence and Connor watched them inch down the path, weighted down by the enormous fir.

"They put whipped cream on the hot chocolate!" Alyssa called over her shoulder.

"Real whipped cream!" Emma added.

Connor laughed as the tree began to bob along at a faster pace—no doubt propelled by Sarah's eagerness to get her idealistic charges away from his cynical self.

The engine wouldn't turn over.

Sarah tried turning the key again and heard…nothing. Not a sputter or a growl or a complaint.

Her forehead thumped against the steering wheel. Now what?

The tree leaned against the back of the van, waiting for one of the teenage boys to tie it on. She'd had the presence of mind to warm up the temperamental vehicle for a few minutes so at least they wouldn't have to unload the tree while they waited to be picked up by a more reliable one.

Which, judging from all the answering machines she was getting, wouldn't be anytime soon.

God, I know you made the universe. Jump-starting this old bucket of bolts should be a piece of cake...

Mandi tapped on the window. "You could call my mom," she suggested. "She said she'd be home this afternoon."

Hope bloomed in Sarah, until she remembered Tina drove a compact. Half the size of the tree they needed to deliver.

"I'll try Pastor Phillips again. If we can't get in touch with him, we'll call your mom."

"Look!" Jennifer began to jump up and down, sloshing hot chocolate all over her scarf.

A black SUV rumbled down the narrow road, the tires chewing up snow and gravel like a tasty afternoon snack.

Sarah groaned. "Girls, don't..."

A chorus of excited shrieks drowned her out and all four girls dashed into the path of the oncoming vehicle.

Chapter Eight

Just as the opening credits of Sarah's life began to pass in front of her eyes, the SUV ground to a stop. The window scrolled down.

"What's the trouble, ladies?" Connor's head poked out and the wind took advantage of the moment, playfully tousling his tawny hair.

I ask for a jump-start, Lord, and you send me Connor Lawe. Am I being punished for something?

"The van won't start."

"And we have to deliver this tree."

"Can you take it?"

"And us?"

Distracted by the girls' nonstop chatter, it took Sarah a few minutes to notice the Christmas tree tied to the roof of Connor's vehicle. A fragrant balsam smaller than the one they'd chosen but almost as round.

Connor jumped out and eyed the Fraser. Even though they'd run it through the baler, it still looked like the first cousin to a Sequoia. "I think there's room for both of them."

His obvious reluctance was lost on his fan club, which performed an impromptu cheer and enveloped him in a group hug.

In less than ten minutes, Connor had the trees secured side by side on the roof. His shuttered expression as he and Sarah got into the car didn't invite questions about the destination of the stout little balsam. In fact, he seemed almost *embarrassed* at having been caught with it.

"It's a good thing you came along to rescue us, Mr. Lawe." Jennifer chirped from the backseat.

"We would have been fine, Jen—" Sarah was cut off by the click of Mandi's chattering teeth.

"My feet were *freezing*. I probably would have gotten frostbite."

"I don't think it's *that* cold." Sarah frowned, wondering why the girls were gushing over a simple ride to town. Granted, they might have been stranded at the tree farm a little bit longer, but still…

"I heard you ask God to help us, Sarah." Emma chimed in. "Isn't it nice that He sent Mr. Lawe?"

Sarah gulped.

Connor's knee jerked and the vehicle bucked as his boot landed an unexpected punch to the gas pedal. "I'll drop you off at the church."

Sarah didn't have a chance to correct him. Not with eight darling little pierced ears tuned into their conversation.

"We're not going to the church," Jennifer said.

"You're not?" Connor slanted a look at Sarah. "From

the size of that tree, I figured it was going in the sanctuary at Lakeshore Community."

"It's for the Carmichaels. We're going to surprise them with it and help them decorate it. When are you going to decorate your tree? Maybe we could help you, too."

Sarah opened her mouth to squash Jennifer's suggestion but got distracted by the color that crept out from the collar of Connor's coat and lit up the five o'clock shadow on his chin.

"That's a great idea," Alyssa said. "Mr. Lawe helped us, so we can help him."

"It's not my tree." Connor's shuttered expression warned Sarah not to press. The girls, however, would give any seasoned reporter a run for his money.

Emma leaned forward between the seats, her blond hair swishing back and forth like a curtain. A wide smile split her round face. "You bought it for them, didn't you?"

Sweet Emma, Sarah thought. Always believing the best of everyone...

Connor's shoulders rolled in time with the sigh that escaped his lips. But he didn't answer.

Sarah blinked. "It isn't for the Carmichaels?"

He shot her an impatient glare but the color in his face deepened.

"Is it?"

"It's just a tree," he muttered.

A bubble of laughter burst inside Sarah. He might view it as just a tree, but Sarah saw something else.

A man who wasn't as tough as he pretended to be.

* * *

The Carmichael family ended up with Connor's balsam. It was either that or lop three feet off the bottom of the Fraser fir to get it to fit in the tiny living room.

The girls spent an hour making paper chains and snowflakes with Beth and Bryan, Francine's older children, while Francine chose the perfect spot on the tree for the glass ornaments she'd carefully unpacked from a cardboard box.

Connor had been planning to slink away the first chance he got, but Sarah's "angels" wouldn't let him. He was the only one tall enough to put the star on the top of the tree. And string lights around the upper casing of the windows.

Two hours later, he was still there, trying to force the children's delighted laughter to bounce off his heart instead of soaking into it.

He glanced at Sarah and then wished he hadn't. She sat in the rocking chair, cradling Francine's baby, Willa, as if she were posing for an artist's rendition of a Madonna and child.

She looked perfectly content. No fidgeting. No impatient glances at the clock like the ones he'd been guilty of as the minutes ticked away, engulfing his entire Saturday afternoon. She'd settled into the slow, rhythmic nod of the rocking chair as if nothing else existed but comforting Willa and giving her mother a chance to concentrate on her other children.

Sarah's hair had pulled free from the elastic band holding it in place and spilled over her slim shoulders.

Hints of amber glinted in the russet curls, reminding him of the sunsets over Jackson Lake.

Don't be an idiot, Lawe. You're a journalist, not a poet.

"Mr. Lawe?" Francine sidled up to him, a spoon in her hand.

He smiled at her, grateful for the opportunity to focus his attention on something other than the woman in the corner. "Call me Connor."

Since the girls' noisy arrival, the weary lines around Francine's eyes had softened a little. Funny. His had gotten deeper! "I'm making fudge. You were voted to be the official taste-tester."

Connor didn't have to ask by whom.

He took the spoon and nibbled at the chocolate on the end of it. "It's great."

"Really?" Francine looked pleased. "It's my mother's recipe. I'll send some home with you and Sarah."

Connor sucked a hunk of chocolate into the wrong pipe and started to choke.

We're not…*together*, he wanted to say. And he would have. If his throat hadn't been burning. And if Jennifer hadn't appeared, with Bryan clinging to her back like a monkey.

"Sarah loooves chocolate," Jennifer said as she breezed past.

Francine smiled. "She's a special person. You're lucky to have someone like her."

"She's not—"

"Sarah is the *best*. Isn't she, Connor?" Now it was

Mandi who stood beside him, nudging him with her elbow.

Connor risked another look at Sarah. Not realizing she was the topic of their conversation, her lips moved as she sang a song to Willa, whose blue eyes remained fixed on the woman who held her.

Silently, he mapped out Sarah Kendle's life. She'd spend the rest of her life in Jackson Lake. She'd make a living putting other people's photos in albums and never care if her own talent was recognized. She'd marry someone local and have a house with a picket fence and half a dozen red-haired babies.

Marry someone who had the same dreams she did.

Willa waved a chubby fist in the air and then her tiny fingers uncurled to pat Sarah's cheek. Sarah pursed her lips and gave them a noisy smack, rewarded by a happy gurgle of laughter.

Connor's breath snagged. He launched to his feet, almost tipping over the chair. Which caught Sarah's attention.

"Is it that time?" she asked.

What time? Time to leave before he put himself in that picture? Leather recliner. Fire crackling in the fireplace. A Labrador retriever bringing him his slippers. And Sarah…

"I have things to do." *Like run for cover.*

"We should leave, too. I promised the girls' parents I'd have them back by five and I know you have to get ready for work." Sarah carefully eased Willa back into her mother's arms.

"Thanks," Francine whispered. "I can't remember when my kids laughed this much."

"I'll call you soon," Sarah promised.

"Here, Francine." Jennifer, always the spokesman, handed her a piece of paper. "All our phone numbers are on it. We happen to all be *great* babysitters. And we give discount rates to our friends."

Tears brightened Francine's eyes. "I'll keep that in mind."

Connor found himself caught in the stampede out the door. Parked behind the SUV was the church van, with Pastor Phillips at the wheel.

"Looks like you don't have to play chauffeur."

Sarah looked relieved. "I'm glad he got it running again. I wasn't sure how to transport the girls without it."

Pastor Phillips got out to greet them and ushered the girls inside the vehicle. "I think it's my turn to drive," he told Sarah. "I just picked this bucket of bolts up from the mechanic and thought I'd see if you were still here." He gave Connor an easy smile. "Connor. How's your dad?"

"Kind of like that van," Connor said dryly. "Ornery. Temperamental. Refuses to retire."

"Sometimes that's a good sign." Pastor Phillips grinned and then turned his attention to Sarah. "Lydia mentioned you were willing to volunteer for the live nativity this weekend."

"Only if I can bring my angels." Sarah laughed.

"I think we can arrange that. I'll give you a call tomorrow." He reached out his hand and grasped Connor's. "It was nice to see you again."

"I almost believe he meant that," Connor mused as the van rumbled down the street.

"He did." Sarah rolled her eyes. "You are so suspicious of people. Did someone put a lump of coal in your Christmas stocking or something?"

Or something. Maybe it had come from seeing poverty so deep that the Carmichaels' house looked like a mansion. Or from watching mothers younger than Francine walk miles to get food and medical care only to be turned away because everything was gone. Maybe it was being haunted at night by the heart-wrenching images of children huddled together under a bridge, with no flicker of life in their eyes.

"Thank you." Sarah touched his arm and even through the thick fabric of his coat, he felt a jolt of electricity.

"For fogging up your rose-colored glasses?"

"For driving us over here. For staying a while. For the tree."

His nerve endings continued to dance after she withdrew her hand. "Speaking of trees, what am I supposed to do with that monster tied to the top of my car? Which, by the way, I can't believe you thought would actually fit inside that little house unless you cut a hole in the roof."

"We did underestimate the size a little bit."

"A little bit."

Sarah grinned. "Wait a second. I think I know someone who needs a tree."

"Who?"

"You'll find out. Just get in the car."

Chapter Nine

"You've got to be kidding me."

Connor killed the engine. He'd patiently followed Sarah's directions until they'd pulled up in front of the two-story brick house on one of the streets overlooking the lake. A very familiar house.

"I'll bet the ceilings are really high." Sarah struggled to keep the laughter out of her voice.

"Not that high," Connor muttered, twisting in his seat to look at her. "He's going to throw us back out into the cold if we try to haul that tree inside."

"He's your father. And you're living there, too, aren't you? I doubt he'll throw you out."

"It wouldn't be the first time."

"You don't have a tree, do you?" Sarah unclipped her seat belt and opened the door a crack.

"That would be because we don't *want* one."

At his frosty tone, Sarah almost lost her nerve. She'd followed God's nudge again. The same one that had led her to give Connor the Isle Royale photo.

"Maybe it will cheer your dad up." Maybe saying the words out loud would convince her, too.

There was a moment of absolute silence. "Have you actually *met* my father?"

"Of course I have." As Sarah jumped out of the car, Robert Lawe's face loomed in her mind. He would have been considered a handsome man if the combination of his formidable jaw and icy gaze hadn't worked in tandem to create a perpetual scowl, as if life was something to be tolerated, not enjoyed.

"Let's go, then."

For some reason, the sudden amusement in Connor's voice unnerved Sarah more than his sarcasm.

"Is this the house you grew up in?" Sarah gasped as they dragged the tree up the shoveled cobblestone walkway to the front door.

"Yes."

"It's listed on the historic register, isn't it?"

"I guess so. My great-grandfather built it in 1908. The year Jackson Lake officially became a town. And I use the term loosely."

Sarah felt a twinge of envy. Generations of a family living in the same house for almost a hundred years.

"Five bedrooms. A formal dining room. Two living rooms. A music room." Connor ticked off the house's attributes like a seasoned realtor. "Great-grandpa built it to impress his future bride and they proceeded to fill it with children. Seven of them. I'm surprised Dad hasn't sold it and bought into one of the new condos on the lake. This is way too much house for one person and he hasn't exactly kept the place up. Mom loved every crumbling brick—"

"That's probably why your dad hasn't sold it."

They'd reached the front steps and Connor dropped the tree, peering at her over the branches. "What?"

"If your mom loved the house, that's probably why your dad can't sell it," Sarah repeated.

"There's just one flaw in your theory. My father doesn't have a sentimental bone in his body."

"So you admit it's a flaw." Sarah grinned.

A reluctant smile tugged at Connor's lips. "I hate to burst your bubble, Pollyanna, but my dad hasn't sold the house because he knows no one in their right mind would buy it. It's hot in the summer. It's cold in the winter. It's—" Connor paused to shoulder open the door.

"Beautiful." Sarah breathed.

Keeping in mind who owned the house, she'd expected something cold. Austere. A hundred-year-old piece of history stripped of its charm by vinyl tile, drywall and dropped ceilings.

Instead, a flagstone floor in muted shades of brown graced the wide foyer. The sunlight had faded the wallpaper—embossed with tiny ferns—to a comforting shade of green. Time had dimmed the luster of the original crown moldings but they hadn't lost their warm glow. Even in its quiet elegance, there was a friendly solidity to it. It was the type of house that could stand up to children and dogs. To spills and slammed doors. To music and laughter. The type of house that invited *living*.

Not the kind of house she'd expected Robert Lawe to

own. If she'd grown up here—had looked at the world from these windows—she never would have left Jackson Lake.

Sarah caught a glimpse of her reflection in the antique oval mirror above the umbrella stand and winced. The pine needles and twigs stuck in her hair made her look like a red-headed porcupine. "Maybe I should use the servant's entrance in the back?"

"Don't worry. By the time Dad gets through with us, we'll look a lot worse." Even as he spoke, Connor reached out to pluck a pine needle from her hair.

Sarah sucked in a breath as he tugged on one of her curls and let it glide between his fingers. He stilled, his quicksilver eyes staring down at her. Searching for something.

"This is crazy," he murmured.

He wasn't referring to the Christmas tree. Sarah agreed but it didn't stop her heart from performing a brief gymnastics routine inside her chest. She couldn't be attracted to Connor. That old cliché "opposites attract" was based on temperament. Not on dreams for the future. Or values.

"What's going on?" A voice bellowed, severing the fragile connection between them. "Close that door! I keep the doctors busy enough with my bad heart—I don't need pneumonia, too."

Sarah and Connor stepped apart like two guilty teenagers caught in the porch light. Connor yanked the rest of the tree inside and pushed the door shut with the toe of his boot.

"What's that?" Robert glared at the Fraser, wedged between the walls of the foyer like a cork in a bottle.

"It's a tree, Dad."

"I know it's a tree." Robert gave Connor a withering look. "What is it doing here? In my house?"

Connor shoved his hands into his coat pockets and shrugged. "Ask her."

Oh, thanks a lot, Sarah thought. One more reason to blame that unexpected, lightheaded fizzy feeling on the sudden change in temperature from outside cold to inside warm.

Robert's gaze swung to her and his eyes narrowed. "Sarah Pendleton...Pendle."

"Kendle." Shocked by the change in Robert's appearance, Sarah forgot to be intimidated by the man. He'd lost a fair amount of weight since the last time she'd seen him. The hollows beneath his eyes were deeper than she remembered. His skin had a yellowish cast and hung in rumpled folds from his prominent cheekbones. Only his eyes hadn't changed—they still burned with life. And they happened to be the same shade of January gray as Connor's. "We had a leftover tree, so we thought we'd bring it here. Connor mentioned you didn't have one yet."

Connor lifted his eyebrow at the emphasis she put on the word *yet.*

"I don't want a Christmas tree. They're nothing but a hassle. Silly tradition if you ask me," Robert ranted. "I hope you didn't have to pay by the *foot* for that monster. If you did, it's coming out of your inheritance, Connor. I suppose the only room it'll fit in is the music room.

Don't just stand there gawking…" Robert pivoted and headed back down the hallway.

Connor's mouth opened but no sound came out.

Sarah grabbed a sturdy branch near the trunk and gave him a bright smile. "You heard your dad. Quit gawking and bring the tree to the music room."

Connor hadn't set foot in the music room since he'd been home. Partitioned off from the more formal living room by French doors, it welcomed people like a friendly hug. The narrow-paned windows in the house were stingy about how much sunlight they let in, but not in this room. Floor-to-ceiling windows made up three of the walls, each framed by a patchwork border of stained glass. The furniture, as spotted from age and sun damage as an old woman's hands, was still covered in girlish pink damask. The ancient upright piano he'd pounded on as a child lived out its dignified retirement in the corner.

It had been his mother's favorite room.

Connor remembered Robert teasingly referring to it as her "sanctuary." Without closing his eyes, he could see her teacup with its matching saucer on the coffee table. Her book of daily devotions stacked neatly on top of her Bible, always within reach. Funny how he'd never thought of his mother in terms of her faith before. He'd been without a permanent residence for so long he'd forgotten that in the ten years he'd lived under Natalie's guidance, she'd created a home for the three of them, overflowing with laughter and love.

A conversation he'd overheard between his parents

returned as clearly as if had taken place the day before.
On a rainy Saturday afternoon he'd entertained himself
by playing James Bond and ended up hiding behind the
old steamer trunk his mother stored blankets in.

"I don't know how you can call it a music room when
you won't even let me put a radio in here," Robert had
complained.

"I like the quiet." Natalie laughed softly. "Besides
that, we don't need a radio, Robbie. We can make our
own music."

"I like the sound of that."

Connor peeked around the trunk just in time to see
Robert—known for his brooding reserve—playfully
sweep Natalie into his arms and bend her over his arm
in a low dip.

And even though he hadn't been included in their
embrace, Connor felt as if he had. For some reason, witnessing that private moment between his parents made
him feel secure. Loved. It had made it easier for him to
reach out to his dad, a man who found it easier to give
instruction than encouragement.

Natalie could coax things out of Robert that most
people never saw. Laughter. Whimsy. An impromptu
game of baseball in the backyard. A family outing to
scout for the perfect tree. A tree they'd put in this very
room...

"Connor! Wake up and give the young lady a hand.
If she falls off that chair, she'll break a leg and probably sue us for every penny we've got."

Sarah's gurgle of laughter shocked Connor to the
core. He'd seen grown men run sobbing from the room

after ten minutes in Robert's company when he was in one of his moods.

"I don't break very easily, Mr. Lawe. In fact, I'd probably *bounce* if I fell off the chair. Flannel-lined jeans and too many Christmas cookies." She pushed her hands over the contours of her slim hips and Connor decided to check the thermostat to make sure it was working. The house felt a bit warm.

"It's going to scrape against the ceiling," Connor predicted as he and Sarah fought to get the tree vertical.

"It's not that tall." Sarah gasped as the top of the tree scraped a trail through the paint on the ceiling.

"You should have cut some of the trunk off first. And you need a tree stand. Unless you plan to leave it propped up in the corner."

Connor glanced at his dad, who'd settled into one of the wingback chairs to play foreman. "Thanks for the tip."

"Do you have ornaments, Mr. Lawe?" Sarah kept one hand braced against the trunk. Not that her weight would prevent it from falling over if it took a notion.

"If I never bother with a tree, why would I have ornaments?" Robert grumbled. "There might be some in the storage closet under the stairs. Call me Robert."

Connor grabbed Sarah's hand and yanked her out the door. "Do you realize what you've gotten us into? Now we're going to have to decorate it."

"You make it sound like I got us embroiled in a plot to overthrow a foreign government."

"A little closer to my reality."

"That's just sad."

"There is a world beyond the utopia of Jackson Lake, you know," Connor felt the need to point out.

"I've seen it."

He kept forgetting that. It was easier to imagine Jackson Lake and Sarah as a matched set from the beginning.

What if she'd gone to high school with him? What if they'd met at Roscoe's after a football game and fallen in love over hot fudge sundaes? Would he have stayed?

The thought blindsided him and Connor fought back with his best argument. It was a moot point. After his mother's death, his dad had checked out as a parent. *The Jackson Lake News,* trapped in a lost episode of *Mayberry R.F.D.*, was destined to be swallowed up by one of the larger dailies. He couldn't change the past. He *had* left. And he had no intention of coming back. There was nothing to come back to.

Sarah's piercing shriek drilled a hole through Connor's eardrums.

He jerked, bumping his head on the low ceiling of the closet. His first thought was "spider." He'd seen a few scuttling for cover when they'd started their search for the elusive box of Christmas ornaments.

"There's something…furry…in here."

"Something alive?"

"Think about what you just said. It's furry. Whether it's alive or dead really isn't the issue here." Sarah edged away from the box.

Connor sighed and crawled across the space separating them. The closet under the stairs was a dark, four-foot tall obstacle course made up of old rugs, towers of cardboard boxes and discarded furniture.

"Don't get bit," Sarah whispered.

Connor tried to discern what lay in the murky depths of the box. He gave the box a little shake and saw gleaming topaz eyes.

"I think it's a…" He reached in, aware Sarah had crowded closer. The mix of fresh evergreen and the floral scent she wore stirred the musty air.

He yelped and doubled over.

"Connor! What is it? Are you—"

"It's…" Connor groaned as Sarah tugged on his arms. "It's a…teddy bear."

He held out a fistful of something with nubby golden-brown fur and a frayed plaid ribbon.

Sarah plucked the stuffed animal out of his hand and hit him with it. The bear's head wobbled and its pink-stitched mouth smiled at her. She cuddled it against her chest. "You are so…wait a second, is this yours?"

"No."

"Aren't you an only child?"

"What does that have to do with anything?"

"Just for the record, Mr. Lawe, I'm totally on to your answer-a-question-with-a-question strategy," Sarah said. "What's his name?"

"*It* doesn't have one."

"If you don't tell me, I'm going to leave you to decorate that tree all by yourself. Come to think of it, your dad might help you."

Connor's eyes narrowed. "You wouldn't dare."

"Try me."

"I can't remember."

Sarah inched toward the door on her knees.

"Fine. You win. It's Mr. Bear."

"Mr. Bear? That's the best you could do?"

"Hey, I never claimed to be Steven Spielberg or George Lucas. Now throw it back in the box and help me find those ornaments. At the rate we're going, we'll be here until midnight."

Chapter Ten

Sarah lifted an oak frame out of a box and wiped away the dust with the tips of her fingers. A family smiled back at her. A much younger Robert Lawe, his arm curved around a slim, attractive woman with a tow-headed toddler propped on one hip.

She tucked the frame to one side and rifled through the rest of the box. Dozens of photographs. Robert and Natalie's wedding. Holidays. Candid shots of Natalie on her knees in the garden. Stenciling sailboats on a bed-room wall. Playing with her son. Instead of celebrating memories of a woman who had obviously been a cherished wife and mother, someone had stuffed them away in a closet, entombed in a tattered cardboard box.

"Did you find the ornaments yet? I'm beginning to think they're like the Holy Grail. They don't exist."

"No." Sarah swiped the frame against her thigh and set it aside. "I found some pictures of your mom."

Out of the corner of her eye, she saw Connor freeze.

"You have your dad's eyes but you definitely inherited your mother's smile." She held out the frame.

At first, Connor resisted. But then he reluctantly took it from her. And looked down at it.

Progress, Sarah thought, remembering how he'd responded when Alice had given him a snapshot of Natalie.

"How old were you when she died?"

"Ten. But I barely remember her."

No wonder, Sarah wanted to say. Everything that would have helped Connor keep his mother's memory alive had been shoved in a box and hidden away.

Silently, Connor sifted through the photos in the box while Sarah continued her search for the ornaments. Finally, she found a wooden crate brimming with garland. Underneath it, several large boxes marked Fragile.

"We're in business." Sarah turned and saw Connor still absorbed in the photos.

"You really take people's photos and make them into those scrapbook things?" he asked.

One of these days, Sarah thought, scrapbooking was going to get the respect it deserved. "Uh-huh."

"Can you do it with these?" He gestured at the box.

"Sure."

"I have no idea what to give my dad for Christmas. Other than the usual stale fruitcake and silk tie, of course."

"You want it by Christmas?"

She'd looked in that box. There had to be close to a hundred photos jumbled together. One scrapbook page could take several hours to put together. She already had two albums she'd been hired to complete by Christmas.

"He might like these organized into an album. If

not, he can put it in a box that won't take up so much space in the closet."

The hurt was there. She could see it in Connor's eyes. Hear it in his voice. Someone had told her once that when things get buried alive, they stay alive. Robert had buried his pain by becoming obsessed with his career. And he'd modeled that for his son.

Sarah saw the next two weeks flash in front of her eyes. Good News-grams. Decorating. Baking. Taking care of the rush of last-minute shoppers. Running on six hours of sleep. Turning a humungous box of photos into a keepsake.

She felt that nudge again.

"No problem. I can have it ready by Christmas."

During the course of the evening, Connor watched Sarah completely charm his cantankerous old father. When she couldn't get him out of the chair to help them decorate the tree, she handed him strings of tiny white lights and badgered him until he agreed to untangle them. Despite their protests, she plugged in the portable radio from the kitchen and found a station that played nothing but Christmas carols. At one point, she announced she was starving and came back from a foray into the kitchen with a bounty of cheese, sausage, fruit and crackers.

"Hold this, Robert." Sarah handed him the end of a length of red velvet ribbon.

"Pushy girl." Robert snarled and grabbed hold of the ribbon. "Where'd you come from anyway? You don't have any family in the area, do you?"

Connor saw the shadow that skimmed across Sarah's expressive face. And then she smiled.

"As a matter of fact, I do." Sarah began to weave the ribbon through a rope of artificial greenery. "At Lakeshore Community Fellowship."

Connor winced. Now she was in for it. His father had always been suspicious of church. And people who went to church.

"Natalie went to church there."

Connor almost dropped the glass ornament he'd been about to hang on the tree. He hadn't heard his mother's name pass his father's lips for years.

Sarah nodded. "People still talk about her."

"They do?" Pain sawed a rough edge against the words.

"I've heard her voice was as beautiful as her spirit. According to the plaque in the choir room, the pipe organ was donated to the church in her memory."

"Really." Robert coughed. "My fingers are cramping up. Are you almost finished with that?"

Connor blinked as he watched a red stain work its way into Robert's hollow cheeks. The most color he'd seen in his father's face since he'd come home.

"Dad? Are you feeling okay?" he asked cautiously.

"Fine." Robert barked the word.

"Your cheeks are red. Did you forget to take your blood pressure medication today?"

Sarah reached out and gave Robert's arm a friendly pat. "Oh, it's not his blood pressure. It's definitely genetic, though. Acute embarrassment caused by sentimentality. You suffered from an episode this afternoon when Emma realized you bought the Carmichaels a tree."

Sarah pretended not the see the look that passed between the two men. As if they'd just discovered a suspicious package under the coffee table and were trying to strategize the best way to safely dispose of it.

"I'm going to bed," Robert announced.

"And I've got some phone calls to make. I should probably take you home," Connor chimed in.

Pathetic. The both of them. Apparently denial was another condition they shared. As anxious as they were to get rid of her now, she couldn't leave before the final, finishing touch.

"We can't forget the most important part." Sarah flipped off the lights and smiled in satisfaction as the hundreds of tiny white lights nestled in the branches took over. They illuminated the entire room and were reflected in the rainbow of glass ornaments that cast warm puddles of color on the hardwood floor.

"Since you two seem to have forgotten the basics of celebrating Christmas, I should remind you to plug the tree in every evening. Turn the lights out. Sip a cup of hot chocolate. And enjoy it."

"Pushy." A half smile played at the corner of Robert's lips and he lowered his voice to a whisper. "You remind me of her."

She took advantage of the moment to kiss the bald spot glowing on top of Robert Lawe's head. "Thank you."

Connor was quiet as they got into the vehicle. They'd only gone half a block when he glanced over at her. "I don't know where you live."

"Oh." Sarah blinked. "Above Memory Lane."

"You live in an apartment?"

"It came with the building."

"No picket fence? No flower boxes on the windows? No dog?"

"A cat. Keebler."

"Mmm."

In the light from the dashboard, Sarah saw him frown. "I had to be practical," she explained. "Starting a business is expensive. I had to sacrifice something along the way. Someday I'll find the perfect house."

"I'll sell you mine for a hundred dollars."

"I'll take it."

"Great. I'll throw in a weekly newspaper, too."

"I wouldn't know what to do with one of those."

"All you have to do is cover city council meetings, report the local gossip and don't misspell anyone's name." The cynic had returned.

"Jackson Lake is a wonderful town."

"Is that why you're hiding out here? So you don't have to engage in the real world?"

"I'm engaged in the real world. Just on a smaller scale than some people," Sarah said. "And from what I've read of your work, you aren't engaged in it, you just observe it."

Connor stomped on the brake and the antilock brakes growled in protest. They'd stopped in front of Memory Lane.

"I never claimed I could change the world," Connor said. "But I don't think hiding is the answer."

Sarah opened the door and jumped out. "But it's okay to run away."

"Running away?" He followed her into the alley to the door that led to her upstairs apartment. "Who's running away?"

"If the Nikes fit…" Sarah bounded up the stairs.

Connor didn't follow her. But then, she hadn't expected him to.

"They're not cooperating."

Jennifer crossed her arms. "They just need more time."

"They still won't look at each other. That has to be a good sign," Emma ventured.

Mandi, who'd become the voice of doomed relationships, flopped into one of the chairs in the youth room. "We've delivered three Good News-grams this week and he wasn't there. I don't think Sarah's letting him know when our deliveries are anymore."

"She's acting weird." Alyssa called from across the room. They'd posted her by the door as a lookout but still close enough to eavesdrop on the conversation.

"She's falling in love," Jennifer said firmly. "Everyone acts weird when they're falling in love."

"If Sarah won't tell him when our deliveries are, how are we supposed to get them together?"

"We need to be more devious." Jennifer heard Emma's gasp. "In a Christian way," she added quickly.

"I don't have time to be devious," Alyssa said. "Homework. Good News-grams. Shopping. The live nativity…"

Mandi's head jerked up. "Jennifer, didn't your dad volunteer to be Joseph?"

"He's Joseph every year because he's the only guy with a real beard."

"And Sarah is Mary."

"Uh-huh—"

"Your dad didn't look very good when I saw him today. He seemed kind of pale."

"He's fine—"

"Standing out in the cold for a few hours wouldn't be good for him," Mandi interrupted. "We should find a substitute Joseph."

"Who would we—"

Mandi lifted an eyebrow.

Jennifer giggled. Emma moaned and put a pillow over her face. Alyssa gave a whoop and spun a circle.

"You're a genius," Jennifer declared.

"And devious?"

"Very devious."

Mandi grinned.

Chapter Eleven

Connor tried to make it to his desk without being seen. Which had become nearly impossible over the past few days. If he so much as stepped out of his cubicle to grab a cup of coffee, staff members swarmed to him like mosquitoes on a bug zapper.

Questions about copy. Questions about upcoming features. Questions about ads and obits and captions. He was glad it was Friday so he'd have the weekend to recover.

He could feel his former life slipping away. The scary part was he didn't miss it as much as he thought he would. Yesterday, he'd found himself actually looking forward to the plate of cookies the Homestyle reporter, judge for the newspaper's annual Best Christmas Cookie Contest, had been bringing in.

You're getting soft.

Soft. As if preprogrammed, his brain instantly downloaded an image of Sarah. And sent a memo to his fingers, which twitched at the memory of the silky feel of her auburn curls when he'd pulled the pine needle out of her hair.

He hadn't seen her since the night they'd decorated the tree, but he hadn't been able to banish her from his thoughts. So much for out of sight, out of mind. Like the Christmas carols he couldn't shake out of his head, she crept into his thoughts at the strangest times. When he saw a young mother pulling her children down the sidewalk in a sled. When he plugged in the Christmas tree in the music room in the evening.

He'd expected her to call him with the weekly schedule for the Good News-grams but when she hadn't, he assumed everyone was concentrating on Christmas preparations. The rush to send a message to a loved one was probably dwindling, pushed out by more important things. Like shopping.

The box of family photos had made it from the closet to the trunk of his car. With the newspaper staff turning to him instead of Robert, he hadn't even had time to drop them off for Sarah to organize yet. He hadn't appreciated the art of procrastination until Sarah Kendle came along. If just thinking about her sent his pulse into overdrive, who knew what *seeing* her would do to him? He wasn't ready to find out.

"Connor. There you are." Cecily's voice snagged him as he tried to slink past the reception desk.

"*Et tu,* Cissy?"

"What on earth is that supposed to mean? I never took French in high school."

"It means I'm a drone. A reporter at the bottom of *The Jackson Lake News* food chain. Why does everyone assume I know what's going on around here?" Connor unleashed his frustration. "Did he put you up to this? The last time I looked at the masthead, Dad was still the editor."

"The last time you looked, your dad wasn't battling heart disease." Cecily's tortoiseshell glasses, the ones that danced from gold chains like a gibbet, trembled in warning as she leaned forward. "He wasn't sitting at his desk all day because he doesn't have the energy to prowl around the building, terrorizing the people who work for him. People who, by the way, happen to love him and don't want to put any extra burden on him. That's why they're coming to you. Not because of a plot to keep you here. Not because they want to. It's because they don't have a choice."

Cecily hissed the last word, puncturing a hole in Connor's defenses. His frustration drained away. "Cissy…" He plowed his hand through his hair. "This is only temporary. I'm trying to get Dad to retire."

"You're trying to get him to sell."

Connor frowned. "Retire. Sell. It's the same thing."

"No, it's not." Disappointment weighted the words. "And until you realize the difference—"

Connor's cell phone blasted out the opening beats of Beethoven's Fifth. He glanced at the screen and smiled. "Excuse me, Cissy. I have to take this one."

"The White House?" Cecily muttered.

"An angel."

She was late.
With Christmas less than two weeks away, Sarah

had extended the shop's hours into the evening so her customers who worked during the day wouldn't have to bring in their lists and expect her to fill them during their half hour lunch breaks.

To save time, she'd donned the blue cotton robe and white sash before she left. Now, driving down The Avenue, she hoped Jackson Lake's lone, full-time patrol officer wasn't lurking in the parking lot by the bakery with his radar gun set on stun. It wouldn't look very good if Mary, the mother of Jesus, was picked up for speeding.

Not that Connor Lawe wouldn't enjoy putting that story on the front page!

Sarah felt a twinge of guilt. She'd been avoiding him. She tried to rationalize the decision not to give him an update on the Good News-grams by telling herself he had enough information to write a short Christmas piece for the paper. The truth was, she didn't want to sort through the confused tangle of emotions she felt whenever she saw him.

Just when she'd decided Connor was like the Grinch, with a heart two sizes too small, he'd bought the Carmichaels a tree and spent an afternoon decorating it. And the way he'd lingered over the family photos...and casually tucked a blanket over his dad's lap...

There's a man in there somewhere who hasn't forgotten how to feel, isn't there, Lord? If anyone can find him, you can. But, if you don't mind, I don't want any more assignments when it comes to Connor Lawe. Someone else can deal with him.

Someone who didn't lose the ability to speak when Connor flashed a rare smile.

She eased her car into a narrow sparking space between Pastor Phillips's pickup truck and Alice Owens's Mercedes. Judging from the noise when she hurried to the stable in back of the church, Will Hopkins had once again donated his arrogant rooster and an entire flock of sheep to make the live nativity…live.

"Sarah! I mean Mary." Jennifer and the rest of the girls barreled toward her, wings flapping. They lined up in front of her for inspection. "We thought you weren't coming."

"I kept the shop open late tonight." Sarah gave each of the girls a quick hug, relieved to see they were already in costume. "Jennifer, why don't you find your dad and tell him I'm here. He was probably getting worried he'd have to hold the Radcliffs' baby."

"Ah…not really."

"Good. Let's go." Sarah linked arms with Emma and Alyssa, greeting shepherds and two of the wise men as they made their way to the stable.

Sarah inhaled the crisp evening air and took a minute to appreciate the stars that winked in the velvet sky above them. She'd spent so much of her life in the wilderness, she felt closer to God when she was outside than anywhere else.

She didn't mind the numbness in her toes. Or the chill that had already breached the thick wool of her mittens. Despite the chaos of the initial setup, in half an hour the only noise would be the occasional ad-libbed bleating of the sheep as everyone took their places and recreated the Christmas story. People from all over the county would come, separating themselves from their busy lives to become part of the Christmas story and reflect on the words Jennifer had been enthusiastically proclaiming for the past two weeks. *I bring you good news of great joy.*

It was part of the reason why she volunteered for the live nativity.

"Sarah, we're going to see Mr. Hopkins's llama," Jennifer said.

"It's almost time to—"

"Be right back!"

Sarah shook her head and rounded the corner of the stable. No sign of Joseph. Or the baby. Maybe because of the steadily dropping temperatures, they'd decided to use a doll instead of four-month-old Benjamin Franklin Radcliff.

She tugged off her mittens and pushed them into the sleeve of her coat, which she hid behind a bale of straw. Staying in character meant no down jackets or Polartec. Mary and Joseph were the only characters that actually fit inside the life-size crèche, which meant they got to take advantage of the tiny space heater hidden inside an old crate.

"This wool is itchy. And I think this baby belongs to you. Although I think someone has a twisted sense of humor. It's one of those Betsy Wetsy-type of dolls and I've got the wet sleeve to prove it."

Sarah turned. Froze. Blinked several times to disrupt the hallucination.

A man, his lean frame shrouded in brown burlap,

stood several feet away. Even with a fake beard glued to the lower half of his face, there was no mistaking those pewter-gray eyes.

"What...why are you here?" she croaked.

"I was wondering that myself. But now, I've got a pretty good idea."

The pint-sized manipulators.

Somehow, during the Oscar-worthy appeal to find a replacement for her father in the live nativity that night, Jennifer had failed to mention that Sarah would be playing the part of Mary.

And the expression on Sarah's face clued him into the fact she was as uncomfortable to discover they'd be sharing a stable for the next two hours as he was.

"Connor! Connor!" The four angels swooped into the stable, surrounding him. "You're here."

"Was there any doubt?"

They nodded happily. Sarcasm was obviously wasted on angels.

"Jen—where is your dad?" Suspicion laced Sarah's ordinarily pleasant tone.

"He wasn't feeling well." Jennifer scuffed the straw with her boot, eyes downcast. "I told him I'd find someone to fill in for him and Connor volunteered."

The girl, Connor thought in amazement, was a budding actress. *Connor volunteered*. Funny how those two simple words put a completely different spin on the truth. Especially after she'd badgered, begged and finally guilted him into agreeing to take part in the live nativity.

"Isn't that great?" Alyssa asked, striking a familiar cheerleading pose and using her mittens as pom-poms.

"Great," Sarah repeated, refusing to look at him. "You girls better take your place by the shepherds now. We'll be starting in a few minutes."

Emma lingered for a moment, peeking up at him through the fringe of hair over her eyes. "After it's over, my mom is serving hot cider and cookies in the fellowship hall. I made the ones that look like candy canes. Can you stay, Mr. Lawe?

Saying no to Jennifer Sands, whose verbal barrage on the telephone that afternoon had reminded him of one of those yappy little dogs who bark until they get a biscuit, had been difficult enough. Saying no to Emma White, with her big blue eyes and floppy golden curls, would be the equivalent of stepping on the tail of a golden retriever puppy.

"If I'm not in the hospital with frostbite."

Sarah's low chuckle cut straight through him. "You can stand by the heater, Joseph."

The girls exchanged grins and dashed off.

Leaving them alone.

"So, how are you doing…stranger?"

Color pinked Sarah's cheeks. Okay, subtle he wasn't. It came with the job. So did confronting people about their secrets. In his conversation with Jennifer, she'd let it slip that they'd delivered three Good News-grams during the course of the week.

He'd been shut out of the loop.

And he was going to take advantage of the next two hours to find out why.

Chapter Twelve

"If Mary and Joseph had this much company, I'm beginning to understand why they fled to Egypt."

"Shh." Sarah suppressed a smile and tried to ignore him. Not that she'd been successful so far. They'd been together for over an hour but the steady stream of people passing the stable had made it impossible to talk. Sarah counted that as a blessing. The glint in Connor's eye told her Jennifer had spilled the beans about their latest Good News-grams. The ones he hadn't been included in.

"Sarah! It's Sarah!" A little girl broke away from the crowd of people and skipped up to them.

Beth Carmichael.

"Hi, Beth." Sarah broke character as Francine's daughter slipped between the rails of the fence separating the stable from the visitors. The one designed to keep the animals in and small children out.

"Look at my new coat." Beth struck a catalog pose. "We all got new coats. Even my mom. Some ladies came over this afternoon and dropped off all kinds of presents...and a turkey. I like macaroni and cheese better than turkey but Mom said—"

"Beth!" Francine caught up to her wayward daughter, her face as red as the stripes in the scarf knotted around her neck. "I'm so sorry, Sarah. I didn't realize she'd know anyone here."

"That's all right. I'm glad you came." Sarah shifted the doll to one side as Beth wiggled right into her lap.

"I know who this is," the little girl said, touching the lifelike hair on the doll's head. "It's Jesus. One of the ladies who came over today read me and Bryan a story about him."

"That's right." Sarah was aware of the smiles and whispers of the people pressing in closer to see this unscripted version of the nativity. "Christmas is the day we celebrate Jesus' birthday."

"Was he really born in a barn? With animals?" Beth looked envious.

"A stable." Sarah nodded.

"Willa was born in a hospital." Beth tugged on Jesus's foot and Sarah got the hint. She eased the baby into Beth's arms.

"The ladies said they brought us all that stuff because Jesus loves us," Beth announced, her clear voice audible in the silence that had descended around the stable. "So I'm going to love Him back." She pressed a gentle kiss on the doll's head.

Sarah swallowed hard, a millisecond from losing it in front of half the population of Jackson Lake. Connor squeezed her shoulder, the warmth of his hand stemming the emotion that threatened to overflow.

"I'm glad, honey," she whispered.

Beth spotted her "angel" friends and with a shriek of delight, scrambled off Sarah's lap and skipped toward them.

Francine hesitated. "The people from church...I didn't expect..." She leaned forward and Sarah hoped she wasn't going to apologize for Beth's behavior. The child's simple declaration of faith had not only touched her but everyone around them. "Thank you, Sarah."

Sarah couldn't find her voice so she nodded. But Francine wasn't done. Her smile was shy but hopeful. "I just wanted you to know...what Beth said? It goes for me, too."

"It can't be that simple."

"It is."

Connor hadn't realized he'd spoken the words out loud until he heard Sarah's soft-spoken response.

He flashed an impatient look, taking advantage of the momentarily lull to peel off a corner of his beard and scratch at the adhesive stuck to his chin. "Life is too complicated."

"Life is complicated," Sarah agreed, surprising him. "That's why God gave us one answer. Jesus. He even told his followers they needed to have faith like a child."

"Accepting everything they're taught without asking questions." Connor's lips twisted.

"Not childish, *childlike*. It's about trust. And coming to God with an open heart. A curious heart. A desire to have a close relationship with our Father that nothing will get between."

Sarah's earnest words burned their way through him. And now he had an image of what she meant. Beth. Who'd come to the conclusion that if Jesus loved her enough to send someone with a new winter coat for her, she was going to love Him, too.

Connor decided the safest thing to do was change the subject. He still had his mother's Bible somewhere in his father's house but he'd never bothered to read it. He'd decided long ago that if God hadn't listened to Natalie's prayers and spared her, he knew God wouldn't listen to him—an angry little boy desperately missing his mother. So they'd stopped talking.

Or maybe, *he'd* stopped listening.

"So, the girls must be done delivering Good News-grams for the year?" He'd learned retreat was sometimes the wisest course of action.

Sarah's quick intake of breath said she was on to him. The look she tossed in his direction called him a coward. "I thought you probably had enough material to write your article."

"Really." He didn't want to admit that as much as Sarah's proximity sent him off balance, he'd actually missed being part of the group. Bracing his poor eardrums for the blast of the trumpet. Seeing the expressions on peoples' faces when the girls sang a familiar Christmas carol.

"We have two more." She gave in. "One on Tuesday. One on Friday."

"That wasn't so hard, was it?"

"Hey, you two!" One of the shepherds waved his

crook at them. "Nine o'clock. Time to punch out and call it a night."

"Speaking of punch..." Connor motioned toward the welcoming lights of the church in the distance. "You're staying, right?"

Sarah shook her head and a curl sprang out from under the scarf. "Tomorrow is Saturday. I've got a class in the morning."

"A class?" Unexpected disappointment arrowed through him.

"A scrapbooking class. I teach them twice a month." She rose to her feet and handed him the doll. "Jennifer and the girls will keep you company."

The last time she'd seen him, she'd accused him of running away. So why did he get the feeling *she* was the one running away this time?

The next morning, Connor found Sarah drowning in a sea of colorful scraps of paper. He took a tentative step into the shop and winced when something crunched under his foot.

"Earthquake?"

"Cub Scouts."

"That was the class you taught this morning?" Connor couldn't help it. He laughed. "You gave boys scissors and glue? On purpose?"

"And paper punches."

"I hope you learned a valuable lesson."

"It seemed like a good idea at the time." Sarah sighed. "They came in to make mini-albums for their parents for Christmas. It taught me to appreciate the girls more. They lack that special ability to turn colored pencils into swords. And javelins."

"Speaking of making albums for parents. I brought you the box of photos." He almost felt guilty giving her another project. Until she smiled.

"Bring them in. I'll be here for a while." Hands on her hips, Sarah surveyed the empty paper cups that had somehow ended up on the floor. "They're definitely not going to earn their recycling badges this year."

When Connor returned several minutes later, Sarah was waiting for him, holding the door open. "Just put them in the back room. Past the register."

Memory Lane, Connor thought as he pushed his way through the narrow space between the card tables Sarah had set up, could replace blood pressure medication. A store that sold rubber stamps and scissors and paper shouldn't be the kind of place that brought a feeling of peace. Tempted a person to relax. With the Christmas tree and homey holiday decorations, the interior of the store looked more like someone's living room than a business.

Sarah paused to reset the CD player, check the level of cider in the carafe and unveil another platter of star-shaped sugar cookies. Her movements were graceful and unhurried, despite the fact her shop had served as a holding pen for a group of rambunctious boys most of the morning.

Maybe, Connor realized, it wasn't the store that reduced stress. Maybe it was Sarah.

He pushed through the colorful fabric panels separating the back room from the rest of the store and almost dropped the box of photos.

"Sarah, there's a mountain lion on your desk. Wearing a Santa hat."

He heard Sarah chuckle. "That's Keebler. My cat."

"I know what cats look like. This is not a cat." Connor eyed the enormous animal staring back at him with unblinking peridot eyes, looking like a fur-covered sphinx.

The curtain brushed aside and Sarah stood beside him. "I adopted him from the animal shelter. He usually stays upstairs in my apartment, but he visits the shop on the weekends. He loves everyone. Although after the Cub Scout troop this morning, he might have changed his criteria to only love people more than five feet tall." She rubbed the underside of Keebler's chin and the cat's eyes drifted shut in absolute contentment. Connor didn't blame him a bit.

"I'd take half a dozen if I had the room. And a dog, too. It would be nice to have them all waiting for me at the end of the day."

Connor set the box down on the floor and reached out, flicking the white pom-pom on the Santa hat with the tip of his finger. "This is probably the reason he's hiding back here, you know. Animals need to maintain their dignity."

"You've had pets?"

"Not unless you count the rat I shared a room with in Thailand. My job takes me away at a moment's notice and I can't worry about leaving someone behind. I don't even have a houseplant."

"Mom felt the same way. She always told me it wouldn't be fair to drag an animal around the country, but that didn't stop me from begging for something... anything. I remember I tried to lure a prairie dog into the car once."

Connor didn't laugh along with her. He had a clear picture of Sarah's childhood and what it must have been like for her to grow up the only child of a famous nature photographer. She'd shared her mother's dream for years, and with her talent she could have easily stepped into Anne's shoes. But given the choice, she'd chosen something else. Her own business housed in a hundred-year-old brick building. A menagerie of pets. A close-knit community. Church. All served up home-style, compliments of Jackson Lake.

In some ways he was like Anne Elliott. A wanderer. Someone more committed to his career than to people. To ask Sarah to leave would be like uprooting a sugar maple and transplanting it in the desert. To ask her to wait would be selfish...

The room blurred and Connor braced one hand against the table for support. Not that it did any good. He still had the sensation he was falling.

For Sarah.

When he came to, Sarah was still talking. "...better back a dump truck in here now and get rid of some of this mess."

"I'll help." He was as surprised as Sarah at the offer. That's what she did to him. She turned him inside out, leaving his heart exposed.

Now would be a good time to run, Lawe. You're only

here on a temporary assignment and Sarah Kendle is a permanent type of woman.

He ignored the voice of reason for the first time and tuned in to his heart instead. Even though choosing to spend more time with Sarah reminded him of the time he'd flown over the Gulf of Mexico while a hurricane bounced the plane in the air like a rubber ball. Exhilarating. Terrifying. A scared-spitless-let's-do-it-again feeling.

"I never turn down help." Sarah hadn't known up until this moment how challenging it was to fake a bright smile. There had to be an article out there somewhere about the correct way to do it.

She'd already spent a restless night thinking about Connor. Praying for Connor. And trying very hard to fight her growing attraction to Connor.

Which was getting harder every time she was with the man. She wished he'd revert back to the frustrating, cynical journalist she'd met at Roscoe's Diner that night. But no. She'd been with him enough to catch fascinating glimpses of a man with an offbeat sense of humor, an unexpected sense of chivalry and a soft heart.

If he insisted on helping her clean up, she'd assign him a task that would take him out of her line of vision. Because at the moment—in his bulky fisherman's sweater and worn blue jeans—Connor was the most eye-catching item in the shop.

"Can you take out the trash?" That would at least put him in the alley behind the building.

The ring tone on Connor's phone suddenly played a jazzy version of "Jingle Bells."

Sarah raised an eyebrow and Connor scowled as he yanked it out of his coat pocket. "It wasn't me. Jennifer changed it last night...hello?"

His eyes darkened. "Where is he now?"

"Connor?" Alarmed by his expression, Sarah instinctively moved closer as he snapped the phone shut.

"That was Cissy. Dad is at the office. He's having chest pains."

Chapter Thirteen

Sarah spent the afternoon sorting through the photos Connor had given her. It took her mind off the fact he still hadn't called her to let her know how Robert was doing.

With every photo she cropped and arranged on a page, she witnessed a tiny slice of Connor's life. Up until Natalie's death, they'd been a happy family. Natalie had tended her home with the same dedication she tended her family. There were as many photos of her in the garden or working on a remodeling project as there were of her snuggling Connor or standing in the protective circle of her husband's arms.

Her heart aching, Sarah compared a series of photos of the family taken at Christmas. Natalie must have been a stickler for tradition because each year the three of them struck an identical pose next to the Christmas tree. Connor changed from a smiling, fat-cheeked baby cradled in Natalie's arms into a mischievous-eyed toddler with an unruly cowlick. Then to a gangly boy with a wide, gap-toothed smile.

Finally, she came to one and drew a sharp breath. A baggy sweater couldn't conceal Natalie's drastic weight loss, a bandana printed with snowflakes covered her head. Her winsome smile hadn't dimmed. But Robert's and Connor's had.

Sarah, who'd spent most of her life studying photos, could see the raw grief in their eyes. The unspoken knowledge that this would be the last time the three of them would pose by the Christmas tree.

Until now, she hadn't known how Natalie had died. Cancer. The same thing her mother had battled. Sarah drew a shaky breath as she remembered the last six months of her mother's life. Anne's physical strength had slowly drained away but her joy hadn't. Watching her mother cling to God—*my stubborn faith*, Anne had called it—had deepened hers. When her mother was gone, Sarah knew God was the only one big enough to fill the empty spaces in her life.

I know people grieve differently, Lord, but Robert was wrong to put away all the memories of Natalie. Connor needed them. They moved on but they didn't move forward. They never let Your love clean out the wound and heal it. Don't let them spend the rest of their lives like this. Remind them that Natalie's legacy wasn't her garden or her house. It was her love for them. And her faith in You.

Sarah looked up and focused on the photo of her and her mother that hung on the wall in her living room. It hadn't been taken in a special place—no towering mountains or liquid gold sunset in the background. What should have been a day filled with sorrow—the day Anne's doctor told her she had to stop traveling and start treatment—had turned into Sarah's favorite memory.

They'd stopped at a wayside to rest and an elderly man, who had no idea who Anne was, offered to take a picture of them. Sarah watched in wonder as Anne, who never let anyone touch her beloved camera, had laughed and handed it to him.

When the film came back, they'd laughed even more. An RV's rusty fender had somehow nosed into the shot. Their feet were blurry. But he'd captured their laughter. Mouths wide open. Eyes squinted against the sun. Cheek to cheek. Hands clasped.

Sarah had been tempted to put the picture away when she moved into the apartment but decided the sting of pain she felt every time she saw it was worth reliving that day. The day Anne Elliott realized that protecting her camera wasn't as important as protecting the feelings of the gentle old man who'd offered to take their picture.

She knew she'd done the right thing by hanging the picture in a place she'd see it every day. The pain had subsided, leaving behind only the sweetness of the memory.

Sarah picked up another photo of Connor's family, filled with a new determination to finish the album by Christmas. Not only for Robert…but for Connor.

"Where do you think you're going? Doctor Parish told you to rest." Which was probably the reason he'd found his dad sneaking down the hall. His dad excelled at being contrary.

"Quit fussing over me. You're as bad as Cissy."

"Why didn't you just yell if you needed something? I would have brought it to you."

"I don't need anything." Robert glared at him. "I was—" His jaw clamped shut.

"You were what? Trying to prove you don't have to follow your doctor's orders?" *Trying to drive me crazy?*

"For your information, since you've decided to sign on as my keeper, I was going to the music room," Robert snarled. "If I have to sit around all weekend, I might as well have something to look at."

"Right. The blinking penguin ornament should entertain you for hours." Connor knew his dad should be in his room. Dr. Parish had ordered Robert to bed rest for the remainder of the weekend while he scheduled tests at the local hospital on Monday. The doctor probably figured it was the only way to get Robert to stay home from work.

When Connor had rushed over to the newspaper, he found his dad, as pale and crumpled as a paper cup, in the chair behind his desk. Robert had started to have chest pains while putting in some extra hours on the upcoming Christmas issue. Cissy, who'd gone to the office to retrieve the gloves she'd left in her desk drawer, had found him.

Dr. Parish had made an office call and sentenced him to house arrest.

He has no idea what it's like to be on deadline, Robert had blustered on the way home. *He can schedule his patients but you can't schedule a newspaper. Life happens...stories happen.*

So do heart attacks, Connor had wanted to say. But he didn't. The fear in Robert's eyes told him the episode had shaken him up...but apparently not enough to keep him in bed.

"Come on. We'll watch the blinking penguin together." He linked his arm through Robert's and matched his slow, shuffling steps as they walked down the hall. Toward the music room.

He helped Robert settle into the loveseat.

"Aren't you going to fluff my pillow?" Robert's unexpected bark of laughter stunned Connor. "Or maybe you'd rather smother me with it."

"The thought crossed my mind." Connor admitted with a lazy grin. "But then I'd inherit this house. And a newspaper."

Robert stared at the fireplace. "I talked to a Realtor last week. He told me he knows of a corporation that's looking to buy smaller weeklies. He thought I could get a decent price."

Connor dropped like a stone into the wingback chair opposite the sofa. Was this a new ploy to make him feel guilty? Because it was working.

"I hate to admit it, but Parish is right. I can't keep up the pace anymore. It's time." Robert cleared his throat. "I already signed the papers. It's going up for sale the first of the year."

"Just like that."

"You don't look happy. It's the reason you came back, isn't it? To get me to retire?"

Sell. Retire. It's the same thing.

No, it's not.

The brief conversation he'd had with Cissy, when he'd complained about the staff looking to him for direction, returned and gave his conscience a hard pinch.

"And you want me to take over. To carry on the great Lawe legacy."

Robert frowned. "Who put that crazy idea into your head? The last thing I want is for you to take over my newspaper."

There it was. *My* newspaper. Robert didn't need him. He'd never needed him. He couldn't wait to get rid of him after graduation and he still didn't want him around.

"I've got some phone calls to make." Connor lurched out of the chair and started toward the door. Just as he reached it, he slapped his hands on the frame, dropped his head and sighed. Call him a glutton for punishment, but he had to know. "Why? Because you think I'd run it into the ground? Because I'll never be able to meet your high standards—"

"Get back here, son."

"I'm not ten years old."

"Then don't act like it."

Connor turned and stalked back, shields in place. "You don't have to explain, Dad. I get it."

"You haven't met my high standards..." Robert cut him off and Connor braced himself for the rest of the assault. "You created your own. And you surpassed them. I've read your articles. Every one of them. You're ten times the writer I'll ever be. You wouldn't run this newspaper into the ground, Connor, you'd keep it going for the next generation. And you'd do a better job than me.

"I knew you better than you knew yourself when you were in high school. You didn't want to stay here. You wanted to see the world. You wanted to make a difference. I read all those essays you wrote for your English class about responsibility and truth and goodwill toward men." Robert's expression softened. "That was your mother's influence. What you're doing is important. It wouldn't be fair to ask you to give up what you love—what you're good at—and step into my shoes. I didn't ask you to do it when you were eighteen and I'm not about to do it now."

"Let me get this straight." Connor's voice thinned. "You badgered me into leaving Jackson Lake…for me?"

"Of course." Robert looked surprised. "Why else?"

Why else?

Twelve years, Connor thought in disbelief. For twelve years he'd totally misunderstood his dad's intent when he'd told him to go and make something of himself. Every time he'd called and made up an excuse why he couldn't come home, Robert hadn't made so much as a peep of protest or regret. After a few years, Connor didn't even bother to make excuses. He just hadn't come back.

"If you sell…" Connor still had a hard time processing everything. "What about the house?"

Robert wouldn't look at him. "I couldn't give this house away. People want new houses. The kind that have those fancy tubs and walk-in closets."

Finding out why his dad had encouraged him to leave gave Connor the courage to say what was on his mind. Finally. He'd disagreed with Sarah when she'd told him Robert kept the house because of Natalie but now he wasn't so sure. If they were digging up the past, he might as well go at it with a shovel instead of a spoon. "It's because of Mom, isn't it?"

Robert's jaw worked and for a second Connor expected a sharp answer or curt denial. But when he spoke, his voice was soft. "She loved this house."

"But you got rid of everything else that reminded you of her." Connor was surprised at the bitterness that leached into his voice. "The pictures. Her garden. And…" He bit back the word.

Robert searched Connor's face and pain creased his face. "And you. I got rid of you. Is that what you were going to say?" he asked hoarsely.

"Actions speak louder than words. And you never said the words. What was I supposed to think?"

Silence weighted the air, made it difficult to breathe. The hiss of the radiator was the only sound in the room.

"I should have proofread Aunt Amelia's advice column more often. She's always going on and on about communication. I might have learned something," Robert muttered. "When you love someone, you want the best for them. And I figured the best thing for you would be to leave Jackson Lake. To put the past behind you."

"You mean Mom."

"No child should have to go through that."

"It might have been easier if we'd gone through it together."

"I didn't know how to do that. I learned a lot from your mother about living, but she never told me how I was supposed to go on without her when she was gone." His dad's eyes, dark with regret, focused on the Christmas tree in the corner. "I've tried to forget."

"That doesn't seem to be working for either of us. Why don't we try remembering instead?"

Chapter Fourteen

"Mr. Lawe, there's a Jennifer Sands on the phone. She says that even if you told me to hold all your calls this morning, you'll talk to her." Melissa Fisher's grating soprano dropped to a whisper. "How did she know that?"

Connor tapped his pen against the desk blotter. Smiled. "I have no idea. But she's right, I'll take the call. Thank you, Mel."

"Hi, Jennifer."

"You didn't show up last night. Sarah was worried."

"She was?" The words were out before he could prevent them. A computer glitch at the paper had him working after hours but he still would have had time to meet up with Sarah and the girls. But he didn't. After the conversation with his dad on Saturday, thoughts of Sarah only added to his confusion.

He'd assumed it would be so easy. Come back to Jackson Lake. Convince his dad to sell the newspaper. Go back to work.

So far, two out of three. His dad had an appointment with the Realtor. His vacation was up the first of the year, which gave him plenty of time to find someone to ease the workload from Robert until the newspaper sold and a new editor took over.

If everything was falling into place, what was causing the restless feeling he hadn't been able to shake for the past two days?

"We delivered a Good News-gram to Mrs. Hunt, the oldest woman in Jackson Lake…she's like, ninety-five years old. Maybe even a hundred. Anyway, we made peppermint taffy with her because she said she used to do that with her girls and Sarah asked if she'd teach us. It was really cool."

Connor understood the significance of the request. At first, he'd dismissed the whole concept of the Good News-grams as a gimmick. Another one of the meaningless platitudes spouted from Thanksgiving to Christmas and then cast aside for the remainder of the year—like the fire-engine-red sweater with a herd of reindeer prancing up the sleeve.

In the past few weeks, he'd begun to see that Sarah's faith was more the action kind than the talking kind. And that was another reason why he hadn't shown up the night before. He'd walked away from God years ago—he hadn't expected God to wait for him to come back. But somehow, Connor had the feeling that He was. Waiting.

And it scared him. And humbled him. Made him question the decisions he'd made. And the ones he would make in the future.

Something his dad had said still nagged at him. When Connor was younger, he *had* wanted to make a difference. But somewhere along the way, when the constant crises and tragedies he'd covered had overwhelmed him, he'd taken a step back and put a wall around his emotions. It wasn't his job to step in and help, it was to take notes. Report the facts.

"So what do you think?" Jennifer asked. "Will you come?"

Connor realized she'd been chatting the whole time. "Where?"

There was an audible sigh. "To our skating party. Friday is our last delivery and we're going to have a party afterward."

"I don't think so." Coward. "I'll be working on the Christmas issue."

"But we're exchanging presents. And I know Emma made something for you."

She'd played the Emma card. Connor stifled a groan. "What time?"

"Seven o'clock. Slader's pond. Do you know where it is?"

Another memory tugged at him. He knew. He'd skated on it as a kid. "I'll be there."

Sarah looked in the mirror and decided the black wool scarf she'd wrapped around her neck coordinated with the circles under her eyes. She'd been up late the past three nights, trying to finish the scrapbook for Connor. She'd also worked on it every spare minute at the shop during the day. There hadn't been many of those considering it was near the end of the Christmas rush.

"I think I'm dressing for the wrong holiday," she told Keebler, who blinked sleepily at her from his spot in front of the heat vent.

She rummaged around in her cosmetics bag for something that would pull the attention away from her bloodshot eyes. She never wore a lot of makeup and the tiny pots and tins she opened had dried up, leaving behind clumps of what looked like modeling clay.

"It's not like he cares what you look like," Sarah muttered, wondering if the tube of raspberry pink paste she'd unearthed was meant for lips or cheeks. "If he even shows up."

Connor had skipped the Good News-gram delivery at the beginning of the week and tonight was the final one. After that, she planned to take the girls ice skating.

She wanted him to be there. And not just so she could give him the scrapbook. When he hadn't shown up on Tuesday night, disappointment had burned its way through her. Especially since he'd given *her* a hard time for not including him the week before.

She'd tried to hide it from the girls, but when Jennifer and Alyssa both asked if she was all right—and Mandi had actually given her a hug when Sarah dropped her off—she realized she hadn't been as successful as she'd thought.

Sarah had spent the rest of the evening rationalizing her feelings. She felt sorry for Connor and his strained relationship with his father. As a Christian, she didn't want anyone to turn away from God, the only one who could truly change a person's heart. They'd formed a tenuous friendship of sorts so of course she'd been looking forward to seeing him.

Right.

She'd finally faced the truth. She was falling in love with him. He'd somehow worked his way into her heart and when he left Jackson Lake, he'd take a piece of it with him. When she occasionally allowed herself to dream about the man she wanted to share her life with, he was a man who shared her values. Her love of small-town life. Her faith. Not an award-winning journalist who wasn't sure God intervened in peoples' lives and who distanced himself—physically and emotionally—from the only family he had left.

Connor's career came first. Even if he stopped traveling, he'd want to live in a big city, not a small town like Jackson Lake.

"We're too different, Keebler." She gave up and applied a thin layer of lip balm. "I'm staying. He's leaving. And it's not like he's shown any interest in me the past few weeks."

If she didn't count the little sparkles of electricity she'd experienced the night they'd brought Robert the Christmas tree. No, when she saw him tonight, she'd smile at him. She'd be his friend. She'd pray for him.

And she'd never forget him.

On her way out the door, Sarah grabbed the scrapbook and tucked it under her arm. She'd left several blank pages at the end. Hopefully, Connor would realize their significance.

It was never too late to start something new. With his relationship with Robert. With his memories of Natalie. And with God.

Connor stared at the keyboard as the popular phrase *been there, done that* coasted through his head. The place had changed—the first time he'd been sitting at Roscoe's—but the struggle was the same. He was still trying to figure out what to do about his warm fuzzy Christmas story.

Stick with the facts. Be objective.

Not exactly the criteria for writing a warm fuzzy Christmas story but it was the way he worked. Only this time it wasn't working. The heart of the story refused to be contained by the facts.

Kind of like another story.

It was the first time Connor's dedication to research had backfired on him. He thought it would be a good idea to start the article with the verse Jennifer always quoted before they delivered the Good News-gram, so he'd asked his Dad that morning where Natalie's Bible was. Even though he'd been doubtful Robert would still have it or that he'd know where it was.

Wrong on both counts. Robert had not only kept it, he'd told Connor it was in the drawer next to his bed.

Connor took the Bible to work with him and thumbed through the gold-tipped pages to the gospel of Luke.

He'd found the verse. And kept reading.

He'd told Sarah that he believed God existed but

wasn't convinced He intervened in the lives of people. But if he accepted the Christmas story, he had to accept his theory was wrong.

Immanuel. God with us.

If God coming to earth as a human—willing to leave His place in heaven and become flesh—wasn't intervention, Connor didn't know what was.

Work with me here, God. It's been a while since we talked. My fault, I know, but this is new ground I'm covering. You'll have to be patient with me. The last time we talked, I think it was the day Mom died. And if I remember correctly, I told You I didn't want to have anything to do with You.

His tentative prayer was interrupted by the winking red light on the telephone on Robert's desk. Connor had stepped in as managing editor while his dad took it easy at home and he'd decided he needed more peace and quiet than one of the cubes provided. So he'd moved into Robert's office. Temporarily.

He punched in a button. "What is it, Melissa?"

"A Carl Davis is on the phone."

Connor's heart gave a sharp kick. He hadn't heard from his boss since he'd come home. He still had a week left of vacation, but he doubted Carl was calling to wish him a merry Christmas.

"Carl. What can I—"

"Get on a plane to London. Tonight. Tomorrow morning at the latest." Carl wasn't much for pleasantries. But then, he couldn't fault him for that. Neither was he.

"I can't leave yet. We've got a double issue that goes to print this afternoon."

"Did I just hear the words *I can't* come out of your mouth?" Carl sputtered.

Connor decided it wasn't as strange as using the word *we*. When had he started to think of the newspaper as a joint effort between him and his dad?

"Have someone else wrap it up. I need you."

Robert needed him, too. But there was more on the line here than recipes for mulled cider and peppermint bark. This was his career. He had enough experience in the business to know there were people hungry to take his place.

"I'll take a flight out on Sunday."

"You're kidding me, right? The airports are packed with holiday travelers. I had to pull a few strings to get you out by tomorrow. The best you could hope for two days before Christmas would be a dog kennel in the cargo hold."

Connor closed his eyes. "I'll see what I can do. But let me make my own traveling arrangements, okay?"

"Just make sure you do."

When Connor opened his eyes, Sarah stood in the doorway. And from the expression on her face, she'd heard enough of the conversation to understand what it meant.

He rose to his feet and padded toward her. She took a step back.

"Hi. I stopped by to give you this." She almost tossed the heavy album into his arms. The flash of disappointment in her eyes nearly undid him.

"Sarah—"

"I have to go."

"Did your boss shorten your lunch break today?"

The joke fell flat but Sarah forced a smile. "I hope your dad likes it." She turned and walked away, the tread of her boots depositing a trail of snow on the carpet.

Connor let her go. What else could he do?

He sank into the chair. Just when he thought life was complicated enough, he'd been called back to the real world. While he waited for the computer to download airline information, he paged through the scrapbook Sarah had put together.

Reliving the first ten years of his life wasn't easy. Every picture stirred a memory. Sarah didn't know anything about his family, but she'd managed to group the photos together with captions and quotes. Her creativity was amazing and he realized she must have dedicated hours to the project. Precious hours carved out of an already busy schedule.

He'd forgotten he'd made a gingerbread house with his mother one year. But there he was, wearing an apron and proudly displaying the finished product. There was another photograph of him and Robert peeking out from under the flap of the tent when they'd camped under the apple tree in the backyard one summer night.

He sucked in a breath when he saw the photos taken during the last year of Natalie's life. Of their last Christmas together. For some reason, he'd assumed Sarah, as sensitive as she was, would have left them out of the album.

But it was time to take his own advice. Instead of turning the page and refusing to feel the pain, he studied the photos. And smiled even as tears clawed the back of his eyes. In every one of the photos, Natalie was touching him and Robert. Clasped hands. An arm looped around the shoulder. He remembered she'd always been a hugger. Somehow, his memories of Natalie had shrunk to the nine months she'd been sick, not the years she'd strengthened the bonds of their family.

She'd be really ticked off about that. And about the way his relationship with Robert had deteriorated over the years.

When he came to the blank pages at the end, he frowned.

An oversight? Not if he knew Sarah. And he did. But he wanted to know her more. Another complication.

Connor scraped his fingertips down his face. And picked up the thread of the conversation he'd been having with God when Carl called.

I have no idea what to do.

The answer came back as swift and as real as if God were sitting in the leather chair across from him.

Now we're getting somewhere.

Chapter Fifteen

He was leaving.

All evening long, the truth chipped away at Sarah's heart. And she realized she'd been hoping Connor would find a reason to stay.

"Sarah?" Jennifer, her arms linked with the rest of the girls, skated up to the wooden bench where she sat. "Can we talk to you for a minute?"

"Of course." That Jennifer even felt she had to ask made Sarah feel worse. Wrapped up in her own emotions, she hadn't been a very attentive leader. It was the last time they'd meet before Christmas and she needed to get out of her funk for the girls' sake.

Jennifer sat down on the bench beside her. "We have a confession to make."

Mandi nodded in agreement while Alyssa chewed on the end of her mitten and Emma sidled closer.

"What's going on?"

"We…we kind of tried to get you and Connor together. And we're sorry. Because you're sad he isn't here tonight. I invited him and I really thought he'd come."

Emma nodded miserably. "You wouldn't look at each other and we thought you *liked* each other and we don't want you to be lonely so we thought he'd be a nice Christmas present."

Sarah blinked. Connor? A Christmas present? What on earth were they talking about?

"We won't try to play matchmaker anymore. We promise," Jennifer said in a rush.

The rest of the girls nodded in agreement.

Sarah pieced the disjointed conversation together and stared at them in amazement. "You thought Connor and I…" She choked on the rest of the words and tried again. "You tried to get us *together*?"

The girls exchanged guilty looks.

"Uh-huh."

"At Francine's."

"And the live nativity."

"And tonight," Jennifer added with a sigh.

Sarah didn't know whether to laugh or burst into tears. She'd been completely clueless to the plot going on right under her nose. "Connor doesn't live in Jackson Lake. He only came to visit his dad." Maybe it was good to say the words out loud. They'd sink in and force her to move on.

"But he could change his mind." Mandi's chin lifted stubbornly. "He likes it here. I know he does."

"We're sorry, Sarah," Emma said. "We didn't mean to make you sad."

"Yeah. We only did it because we love you and you won't always have us around," Mandi said.

Sarah wrapped her arms around the girls and pulled

them against her. "You guys are the best," she murmured. "I'll be fine. But if God wants me to be married, He's got the right man all picked out, okay?"

"Okay." Jennifer exhaled and her breath came out in a puff of frost. "We get it."

"You do like him, though, don't you, Sarah?" Mandi persisted.

Sarah gave a helpless laugh. She wanted the girls to think about others but this wasn't quite what she had in mind!

"Yes, I like him," she said truthfully. "But some things aren't meant to be. We have to trust that God knows what's best for us."

As she said the words, she tucked them into a corner of her heart, knowing they were the only thing that would ease the pain of Connor leaving.

Jackson Lake was going to have a white Christmas. The snow started falling just past midnight and showed no signs of stopping.

Sarah slipped her coat on and searched the pocket for her keys. All she had to do now was turn the open sign around and lock the door. On Christmas Eve, she always closed the shop early so she could attend the special worship service at Lakeshore Community.

Her cell phone rang and a number that Sarah didn't recognize came up. "Hello?"

"Sarah? This is Francine. Listen, I'm at Roscoe's and I wondered if you could swing by for a few minutes."

"Sure. Is everything all right? Are the kids okay?"

Francine's chuckle put her fears to rest. "They're fine. I just need your help with something."

"I'll be right there." She decided to walk the short distance from the shop to the diner. Her car looked like a snowbank and it would take longer to scrape it off than it would to walk. She pushed her nose into her scarf and ducked her head against the swirling flakes.

Even the beauty of the town cloaked in sparkling white didn't cheer her up.

She hadn't seen or heard from Connor over the weekend and since she'd overheard him saying he'd try to catch a flight out on Sunday, she knew he must have left. And he hadn't even bothered to say goodbye.

"Sarah!" The owner of the flower shop across the street waved to her. "Loved Connor's article in *The News*. Next year I'm sending a Good News-gram to my grandmother."

Sarah waved back but didn't stop to continue the conversation.

An issue of *The News* had mysteriously ended up lodged between the doors of her shop on Saturday morning. On the front page, complete with pictures, was the story Connor had written about the girls. It had taken her several hours to gather the courage to read it. When she compared it to the articles she'd read online, she couldn't believe the same man had written it.

With warmth and humor, he focused on the commitment the girls had made to the project and how they'd gone beyond simply delivering a message. They hadn't just talked about God's love, they showed it.

She tried to read between the lines. Was it possible he

finally understood that his view of the world had been colored by his resistance to God? If that was the case, if Connor was allowing God to work in his life, then Sarah knew it didn't matter that he'd left. As long as he found his way back to the roots of his faith. The ones started by Natalie before she died. That was the most important thing and the one she committed to pray for.

There was a closed sign in the window of the diner and Sarah tried the door. It wasn't locked. There was no sign of Bev or Francine when she stepped inside.

"Francine? It's Sarah."

She took a step toward the kitchen but a trumpet blast stopped her in her tracks.

"Behold!" Jennifer, Alyssa, Emma and Mandi stumbled out of the kitchen and stood there grinning at her, dressed in their angel costumes.

Right behind them were Francine and Bev.

And Connor.

Sarah could only stare at him in disbelief as Jennifer lifted her arms and recited the familiar verse.

"This is a Good News-gram," Jennifer intoned. "From Connor Lawe. Because God loves you and—"

"So does he!" Alyssa, Emma and Mandi shouted together.

Jennifer gave them a disapproving look and nodded at Sarah. "That's right. He does love you."

Sarah couldn't move. So Connor did. Two long-legged strides put him right next to her. He put his hands on her shoulders and looked into her eyes.

"I thought you left," she whispered.

"I couldn't leave. Not when I'm currently the proud owner of a hundred-year-old house and a newspaper."

Connor had decided to stay in Jackson Lake? Wait a second. He *loved* her?

"I don't understand. Your career...you don't like small towns."

"I didn't understand it myself. It happened after I took your advice and talked to God. I realized there were more reasons for me to stay than there were to go."

Sarah's eyes began to burn. This wasn't a small thing. Walking away from a job he loved. Staying in one place instead of traveling the world. "What if you get...bored?"

"Bored?" Connor raised an eyebrow at the girls, who'd unashamedly inched closer to eavesdrop. "With this crew hanging around? Not a chance."

"Are we celebrating or not?" Roscoe bellowed from the kitchen. "The hot chocolate is getting cold."

"Don't rush him, Mr. Roscoe," Jennifer called back. "He's slow at this kind of stuff."

The laughter died in Sarah's throat when Connor looked down at her again.

"We haven't known each other very long but I want to change that. Trust me. I'm not going anywhere."

Sarah didn't know what to say. She thought she'd never see Connor again and he was here. For good. For *her*.

"I told you you have to say the words," Jennifer coached him. "It can't come from us."

Connor groaned.

"They need some help. Again." Mandi rolled her eyes.

Emma ducked into the kitchen and returned with Roscoe, who stomped over and held something green over Sarah and Connor's heads.

"Mistletoe." Alyssa grinned.

"*Girls.*" Sarah felt the blush down to her toes.

Connor pulled her close and Sarah gave a squeak.

"They haven't been wrong yet," he murmured.

She looked up. "That's *parsley...*"

Connor smiled. "Use your imagination."

The room and everyone in it disappeared as Connor kissed her. In the background, the girls started to hum. Not a traditional Christmas carol but a cheerful rendition of "Here Comes the Bride."

Connor's arms tightened around her and he lifted his head. The promise in his eyes took her breath away. Then he whispered in her ear.

"What are you doing next Christmas?"

* * * * *

Questions For Discussion

1. If you could send a Good News-gram to someone, who would you send it to? What would your message be?

2. Sarah cut down her own tree and volunteered for the live nativity at her church. What are some of your favorite Christmas traditions? Which ones did you carry over from childhood? What new traditions have you started?

3. How did Connor's priorities change? Was there a time in your life when you had to make a difficult decision about your future? What were the circumstances? What was the outcome?

4. Sarah turned a hobby (scrapbooking) into a career. Do you think she was neglecting the gifts and abilities God gave her by not following in her mother's footsteps as a photographer? Why or why not?

5. What was your favorite scene in the book? Why?

REQUEST YOUR FREE BOOKS!

2 FREE INSPIRATIONAL NOVELS
PLUS 2
FREE
MYSTERY GIFTS

Love Inspired™®

YES! Please send me 2 FREE Love Inspired® novels and my 2 FREE mystery gifts (gifts are worth about $10). After receiving them, if I don't wish to receive any more books, I can return the shipping statement marked "cancel." If I don't cancel, I will receive 6 brand-new novels every month and be billed just $4.49 per book in the U.S. or $4.99 per book in Canada. That's a savings of at least 22% off the cover price. It's quite a bargain! Shipping and handling is just 50¢ per book in the U.S. and 75¢ per book in Canada.* I understand that accepting the 2 free books and gifts places me under no obligation to buy anything. I can always return a shipment and cancel at any time. Even if I never buy another book, the two free books and gifts are mine to keep forever.

105/305 IDN FVW5

Name	
	(PLEASE PRINT)

Address		Apt. #

City	State/Prov.	Zip/Postal Code

Signature (if under 18, a parent or guardian must sign)

Mail to the **Reader Service:**
IN U.S.A.: P.O. Box 1867, Buffalo, NY 14240-1867
IN CANADA: P.O. Box 609, Fort Erie, Ontario L2A 5X3

**Are you a subscriber to Love Inspired books
and want to receive the larger-print edition?
Call 1-800-873-8635 or visit www.ReaderService.com.**

FAMOUS FAMILIES

YES! Please send me the *Famous Families* collection featuring the Fortunes, the Bravos, the McCabes and the Cavanaughs. This collection will begin with 3 FREE BOOKS and 2 FREE GIFTS in my very first shipment— and more valuable free gifts will follow! My books will arrive in 8 monthly shipments until I have the entire 51-book *Famous Families* collection. I will receive 2-3 free books in each shipment and I will pay just $4.49 U.S./$5.39 CDN for each of the other 4 books in each shipment, plus $2.99 for shipping and handling.* If I decide to keep the entire collection, I'll only have paid for 32 books because 19 books are free. I understand that accepting the 3 free books and gifts places me under no obligation to buy anything. I can always return a shipment and cancel at any time. My free books and gifts are mine to keep no matter what I decide.

268 HCN 0387 468 HCN 0387

Name	(PLEASE PRINT)	
Address		Apt. #
City	State/Prov.	Zip/Postal Code

Signature (if under 18, a parent or guardian must sign)

Mail to the **Reader Service:**

IN U.S.A.: P.O. Box 1867, Buffalo, NY 14240-1867
IN CANADA: P.O. Box 609, Fort Erie, Ontario L2A 5X3

FFBPA12

Love Inspired®

SUSPENSE

RIVETING INSPIRATIONAL ROMANCE

Watch for our series of edge-
of-your-seat suspense novels.
These contemporary tales
of intrigue and romance
feature Christian characters
facing challenges to their faith...
and their lives!

AVAILABLE IN REGULAR
& LARGER-PRINT FORMATS

For exciting stories that reflect traditional values,
visit:
www.ReaderService.com